Adam recognized a fire in Eva's eyes. No one cared more for this orchard than Eva.

Adam had fallen in love with this land, too, only he needed to learn how to make it grow and produce a living.

She gestured for ___ ___ how I make the ___

He peered around her shoulder. "Looks easy enough."

"Once you get the hang of it." She turned to look at him, but leaned too far back and slipped. Adam grabbed her arms to keep her from toppling.

She slipped down onto the bottom step, landing on his foot. Her eyes went wide and Adam caught a flicker of panic race across her face. "You can let go."

He stepped back and raised his hands in surrender. "I didn't want you to fall. Worker's comp isn't good on the first day."

Adam smiled, but was curious to know what pulling her close would feel like. He suspected that she'd fit pretty well in his arms.

Books by Jenna Mindel

Love Inspired

Mending Fences
Season of Dreams

JENNA MINDEL

lives in Northwest Michigan with her husband and their two dogs. She enjoys a career in banking that has spanned more than twenty years and several positions, but writing is her passion. A 2006 Romance Writers of America RITA® Award finalist, Jenna has answered her heart's call to write inspirational romances set near the Great Lakes.

Season of Dreams
Jenna Mindel

Steeple
Hill®

Published by Steeple Hill Books™

STEEPLE HILL BOOKS

Steeple
Hill®

Recycling programs
for this product may
not exist in your area.

ISBN-13: 978-0-373-81530-2

SEASON OF DREAMS

www.SteepleHill.com

Printed in U.S.A.

The fruit of righteousness will be peace;
the effect of righteousness will be
quietness and confidence forever.
—*Isaiah* 32:17

To the Frys,
Thank you for sharing your gifts and talents
with those who need them most.
(Especially your cherry pecan bread pudding
shared with the Mindels.)

Acknowledgments

I'd like to thank Randy with Runge Industries Inc
for his time spent answering my many questions
about cherry farming. I hope I got it right!
And the folks at NWMHRS for their
research help as well. My sincere thanks!

To my agent, Karen Solem, for believing
in me. And my editor, Melissa Endlich,
for her encouragement. Thank you both!

To my red-pen-wielding husband,
for his endless patience and support.
You speak my Love Language!

Chapter One

Eva placed a tray of cut dough in the oven and then peered out the window. The wind moaned, making snow swirl against a gray January afternoon sky. The weather might not be as horrible as predicted, but it was bad enough to cancel school on a Friday. In northern Michigan that was pretty bad. As she cleaned off her flour-covered workspace at the island counter, a knock at the door made her jump.

Wiping damp hands against the back of her jeans, Eva crossed the kitchen floor and opened the door. A man with blue eyes the color of laser beams stood on the porch.

"Eve Marsh?" He smiled at her. A devastatingly handsome smile.

"It's Eva." Since when did she sound so out of breath?

He held out his hand. "I'm Adam. Adam Peece."

Eva sucked in the gasp ready to escape. She'd accepted the job he'd offered over the phone this very morning.

"Sorry about not calling before dropping by, but I was on my way to the area and made better time than I thought. Last-minute decision."

Regardless of the high opinion her father had for the guy who'd bought the family cherry orchard, one look at Adam Peece and Eva knew he was not the kind of guy she'd trust. He was too polished, too good-looking, and his fingers didn't look as if they'd ever been dirty.

He grinned as he let his hand drop. "Is this a bad time?"

Eva thought briefly about closing the door on him but backed up instead. "Oh, no. Sorry. Come in and let me take your coat."

He shrugged out of an expensive black wool peacoat, revealing snug black jeans topped by a charcoal-gray sweater. He looked as if he'd stepped off the pages of a fashion magazine. His build was slender but obviously well exercised. The sleek boots gave him the decided air of a European jet-setter.

And this guy wanted her to teach him to grow

cherries? No way. A downstater like him was bound to ruin the orchard, change it or worse—develop it.

He stepped farther into the kitchen. "Something smells incredible."

Eva hesitated.

But her roommate, Beth, who sat at the kitchen table with her second-grade lesson plans, popped up to play hostess. "Eva's famous cherry scones. Would you like one with coffee?"

His grin was quick and brilliant, showcasing even white teeth. "Absolutely."

Eva nearly growled at her friend. Peece was bound to stay if they offered him food, but there was no getting around it. She retreated behind the island counter but not before noticing the flash of interest in Adam's eyes when he looked at Beth. A guy would have to be dead not to notice her statuesque friend. "Mr. Peece, this is Beth Ryken, my roommate."

"Nice to meet you." Adam extended his hand.

Beth took it, and her long blond hair fell around her face, making her look even more angelic. "Have a seat."

Eva might have been dazzled at first—it wasn't every day a male-model type stopped in for visit—but she'd gathered her wits. "Mr. Peece—"

"Call me Adam." He slipped onto a stool tucked under the island counter's generous overhang.

Eva gave him a weak smile. "Since you're here, I can show you what we'll be working on together in February. Pruning tools, the trees…that sort of thing."

"Let him warm up a minute, Eva." Beth gave her a pointed look that said "play nice" as she set down the tray loaded with a coffee service and a plate of scones.

The oven timer buzzed, announcing more scones were done. Eva slipped on her oven mitts. "Excuse me."

"Take your time." Adam poured himself a cup of coffee.

Eva pulled out the cookie sheets and glanced at Beth, who nodded toward their guest. She turned to catch Adam's reaction.

His eyes were closed and a satisfied smile curved his shapely lips. "These are amazing."

His obvious pleasure did funny things to Eva. How could she hold a grudge against a guy who loved her baked goods? Not to mention that she'd agreed to work for him. That should teach her not to accept employment without a face-to-face interview. Not that she had much of a choice after he'd named her wages. She needed the money.

"Made with Marsh cherries," Beth added.

Adam's eyes opened. "Canned?"

Eva set aside her oven mitts. "Dried. They're what's left of last year's pitiful harvest."

"Your father told me about the killing frost last year. Tough loss." Adam stirred cream into his coffee.

Eva clenched her teeth. If only they'd had a bumper crop, it might have made a difference. Instead, Peece had swooped in like a bird of prey sighting a quick kill. He bought up the orchard, enabling her parents to pay off their past-due mortgage and commercial note. Even after leaving the farmhouse to her and giving her brothers money, her folks had enough left over to retire modestly in the Florida Keys. Making everyone happy.

Except her.

Eva shook off the thought. "They're your cherries now, so you can process them however you like."

A moment of awkward silence hung in the air.

And Beth chose that moment to leave. "I have papers to grade, so I'll leave you two to discuss business. Nice to meet you, Adam."

He gave her a wide smile. "You, too."

Eva swallowed the urge to ask Beth to stay. Adam Peece made her nervous. But then so did most men close enough to her twenty-five years of age.

She eyed Adam as he reached for another scone. "Your father said you'd taken the sale hard. I hope we can get beyond that working together."

Eva pursed her lips to stop the sarcastic retort poised for takeoff. Who was he to commiserate?

She felt the corner of her eye twitch as she stared him down. Pretty hard to do when his attention was wrapped up in what he was eating.

"What else are in these?" He held up half a scone and examined it.

"White chocolate."

"Wow. They're really good."

She knew real appreciation when she heard it, but she hadn't expected to be warmed by it. "Now then, Mr. Peece, did you have some questions about the upcoming season? Questions about our conversation this morning?"

His laser blues locked on to her, trapping her. "My father is Mr. Peece. I'm Adam."

Eva looked away. She didn't feel comfortable using his first name. It sounded ridiculous considering hers. Adam and Eva. Cute. Calling him Adam rang so informal and friendly. He'd have to earn her respect and friendship before she doled it out.

"Look, Peece, this isn't easy for me. Working for you on *my* family's farm. It's going to take some getting used to." Tracing the rim of her grandmother's plate with her fingertip, she glanced up at him to gauge his reaction. Would he take offense?

No. In his eyes she read understanding.

Adam smiled at Eva. He liked the way she used his last name. From her it sounded saucy, even though he knew she used it to show that she meant business. He'd expected some reservation from her but not this stark vulnerability underneath a brave front that bordered on cockiness.

Adam leaned back, hooking his knee with both hands. "Working with people, I've gotten used to a lot of smoke blowing. Thanks for being honest with me. I'll be honest, too. I don't want to make this any harder for you. I've got an employment contract for you in the car instead of that fax I sent. After we sign off, I'd like to walk around the orchard on my own."

He'd rushed over here from his town house intent on seeing his land in the dead of winter. He'd seen the lights on in the kitchen of the farmhouse and known he should meet Eva in person. He couldn't wait to get started, discuss the seasonal duties, the whole process. He couldn't afford to waste time. He had one season, *this season,* to prove himself to his father.

"Okay. No problem." Her eyes matched the copper-brown color of her hair and he thought they'd softened toward him. A little.

Adam knew women hit the salons, but Eva Marsh didn't strike him as one of them. She didn't wear a trace of makeup that he could see. She didn't need to. She was small, reaching all of maybe five foot two. And awfully cute wearing an apron covered with embroidered cherries and a smudge of flour on her cheek.

He took a sip of his coffee before he brushed off that flour. "Your father mentioned something about you starting a bed-and-breakfast. When do you plan to do that?"

Eva's mouth had thinned, the softness gone. "For now, that's on hold."

Adam took another bite of his scone. Too bad Eva wasn't as sweet as her baked goods. "Your dad's the reason I hired you. Bob Marsh said you were the best person for the job."

Eva looked straight through him as if measuring him and then finding him lacking. He'd seen that look a million times from his dad, but it still pinched. He wasn't going to let Eva's wariness stop him from learning everything he could from her. With God's help, he wasn't going to let anything stop him from making this work.

Adam nodded. "With the orchard right here, maybe you can do both."

"I'll keep that in mind." Again the impatient glare before looking down at the plate of scones.

The dark fringe of her eyelashes curled against the swell of her cheeks. She had seriously long lashes and a few light freckles on her nose. Then she looked him square in the eye. "Look, I don't mean to be so touchy, but it's been a rough day. My bank shot down my loan application. I need this job and I'll do my best as your farm manager."

Again Adam nodded while something protective stirred deep inside him. He'd erase that furrow in her brow if he could. "Good. I'm looking forward to learning everything I can from you about this orchard. I want our working relationship to be open and relaxed. I'm going to ask you a ton of questions, but I'm committed to an entire season of getting my hands dirty."

She didn't look like she believed him. "It takes more than one season."

"I'm sure it does." After one season, he'd know if acting on his childhood dream was the right direction after so many failed attempts to find his niche. This time his father had thrown down the gauntlet. Success meant Adam could finally walk away from Peece Canning Company. Fail, and he'd lose it all.

Eva brushed a loose strand of her stick-straight hair off her forehead. The rest was tied into a messy ponytail. "Well, I guess we'll have to see how it goes then, won't we?"

Adam knew that was his cue to go get the contract and wrap up this meeting, but he felt an odd urge to stay. Eva's cluttered kitchen was warm and smelled good. It reminded him of his grandparents' farmhouse where he'd spent summers as a kid. That had been the only place where his mom used to bake. The only place he'd ever felt as if he truly belonged.

Adam knew better than to overstay his welcome. When it came to women, Adam never stayed. Not long anyway. "True. Thanks, Eva. It was nice to finally meet you." He hooked his thumb toward the porch. "If you don't mind, I'll get our contract and then take that walk."

He extended his hand.

This time she took it, but when he noticed the softness of her skin, she pulled back. "The snow's deep out there. You're likely to mess up those slick leather boots."

"Thanks, but I have more." He reached for another scone. "Mind if I take one for the road?"

Eva gave him a hint of a smile that revealed a dimple in her left cheek. She was impossibly cute. A real farm girl. "Go ahead."

Adam shrugged into his coat, wondering why he didn't want to leave when Eva Marsh clearly wanted him gone. He went to the door and opened it. Snow spilled in from a good two-foot drift. The snowfall had grown heavier and the wind whipped. "Uh, Eva? I don't think I'm going anywhere."

Eva didn't know what to do with Adam Peece, but she let him stay and watch her bake more scones. He might not be a big man, but he still managed to fill the kitchen with his presence. His classic, defined features begged admiration, and she'd looked her fair share.

After they'd signed two copies of their employment contract, they discussed the first pruning chores of the season. Then Beth had joined them for a quick dinner of leftover lasagna and salad, but Adam still asked a million questions about growing up on a fruit farm. His manners were polished but relaxed and he'd charmed them both.

When he politely excused himself from the table to take a phone call on his cell, Beth leaned forward and whispered, "I think he likes you, Eva."

She rolled her eyes. "Oh, please."

"I'm serious. He keeps checking you out."

"Right." He was probably judging her like she'd taken stock of him. It wasn't as if she was anything to look at wearing an oversize sweatshirt the color of mud.

Beth smiled. "You're lucky he's too short for me, or I might be interested. He's totally yummy with all that dark hair."

"Too long." Eva didn't want to admit that his hair looked good even though he wore it longer than she liked. She'd always gone for the clean-cut, jock types.

"You're crazy," Beth said with a giggle.

Adam entered the kitchen, cutting off their whispers.

"Did you let your girlfriend know where you are?" Beth asked.

Eva shook her head. Her roommate didn't have

a subtle bone in her body. Raised by an indulgent mother and a police officer dad, Beth's practical streak leaned toward saying whatever popped into her head.

Adam laughed as he slipped back into his chair. "I don't have a girlfriend. But I'm supposed to meet up with some friends to ski tonight. My family has a town house at Star Mountain."

Of course he did. That was *the* place to ski, even though it was almost an hour south. She should have pegged him a skier. Eva had never liked the party atmosphere of most slopes, but Adam probably fit right in. His manner might be easygoing, but she sensed intensity simmering beneath that carefree charm.

When Adam aimed his attention on her, Eva felt him tune in as if she were the only woman in the world. It was a heady feeling. And it was no wonder he'd been considered one of Detroit's most eligible bachelors.

She'd searched on Google Adam Peece's name. As heir to the Peece canning kingdom, Adam got around. In the Detroit society columns he'd been linked with models and wealthy downstate socialites and was even rumored to have dated the daughter of a Hollywood actor. Contrary to what her roommate thought, Eva knew a guy like Adam wouldn't give her a passing glance.

"You'll have plenty of fresh powder after today," Beth added.

"Do you ladies like to ski?" Adam ran his fingers through dark hair that ended just below the line of his jaw. *Pretty boy* came to mind, but a deep cleft in his chin took care of keeping his face decidedly masculine.

"No," Eva answered too quickly.

"When I have time." Beth flashed her an odd look.

"What do you ladies do for fun?"

Beth laughed. "Fun? What's that, right, Eva?"

Eva shook her head. "I think I've forgotten."

"Don't you two go out?"

Beth got up from the table, taking her plate to the sink. "I'm getting my master's degree, and ever since Eva's parents gave her this house, she's worked on it nonstop. Painting, putting up wallpaper, you name it."

Adam gaze pierced her. "That's right, the bed-and-breakfast. You've got some stiff competition with the resorts around here."

Eva felt her defenses rise. Pursuing a bed-and-breakfast was perfect considering the incredible views from the farmhouse. Besides, she was a trained pastry chef who wanted to bake on her own terms. "Exactly why I think it will do well. This is a quiet place away from noisy lakeside accommodations and it happens to be surrounded by a cherry orchard."

"And romantic, don't you think?" Beth said. "Perfect for honeymooners, especially when the cherry blossoms are in bloom."

Eva could have clocked her. She didn't want to think of anything remotely romantic when it came to Adam. "We're not far from the beaches. Plus, there are several vineyards nearby."

"Too bad there isn't a ski hill closer for winter business."

"We have cross-country trails on the bike path." Besides, Eva planned to cater to families, couples, honeymooners and other safe people. Not a bunch of rowdy partiers. Not guys like Peece booking her rooms.

He shrugged. "That's cool. It's definitely a play-ground up here."

Considering what she'd read about him, he quali-fied as one of the players. The sound of the wind wailing outside covered a stretch of silence.

"Well, I have to study, so I better get to it. Good night, Adam." Beth made her escape, leaving Eva alone with him once again.

"Want some help with the dishes?" he finally asked.

"Sure." Eva got up from the table. She wasn't about to get cozy with him in the living room, so she might as well let him help her load the dishwasher.

"Who are all the scones for?" Adam handed her a dish.

She stacked plates into the bottom rack. "My aunt Jamee. She's catering a women's group breakfast. I'll deliver them in the morning."

"Where'd you learn to bake?"

She knew he was making polite small talk in an attempt to be nice. But Eva didn't feel nice. The large kitchen that doubled as her office was her favorite room in the house, but tonight his deliciously expensive cologne blended with the oven-warmed air to suffocate her.

Eva let out a short sigh. "My aunt's catering business is where I got my start. I helped her out on weekends when I wasn't needed in the orchard. I love to bake, so I went to college in Traverse City for culinary arts. I worked the resorts awhile and then went to New York City to study pastry. I came home when my folks told me they were selling the orchard."

Adam smiled. "In hopes of talking them out of it?"

Eva's gaze flew to his. Too bad she'd been too late. Not that she could have changed anything. Eva wouldn't hold her parents back from their dreams, even if it meant losing part of her own.

"Your dad told me at the closing that you were

the only one of his kids who'd miss the orchard. He said you have cherry juice pumping through your veins."

Eva shut the dishwasher door too hard and then flipped the switch. "You're pretty chummy with my dad, aren't you?"

Adam shrugged. "Your father's a nice guy. He took the time to introduce me around to the local processors in an attempt to smooth my path. We met several times before and after he agreed to sell."

No doubt the price was higher than her father could refuse. Just like the salary Adam had promised her. After a few months with a steady income, maybe she could try again for that loan.

"Yeah, well, my dad talks too much." *And so do you.*

Adam gave her another soft laugh. "Your father's proud of you. You're fortunate."

Eva wasn't in a count-your-blessings kind of mood. Adam's easygoing charm challenged her fortified walls. Her carefully built up guard. Working for him was one thing. She didn't want to like him, too. "Thanks. Why don't we check out the weather report?"

"Don't worry, Eva. I'll be on my way. The wind sounds like it's dying down. Thanks for dinner. I'll see you in a couple weeks."

Eva nodded as she followed him to the door. The snow had stopped.

Calling Adam Peece an attractive man was an understatement. She didn't look forward to showing him how to run her family orchard, but she'd do her job. It didn't help that Beth's teasing had planted a seed of interest. A seed Eva couldn't let grow.

Chapter Two

Two weeks later, Adam drove the hour commute from his town house to Eva's place. He couldn't wait to get to work—an odd sensation for him. When at Peece Canning, Adam resented each day buried in boring paperwork and dull meetings, no matter how good his head for business might be.

Hands-on work. That was what he'd always preferred. He liked control of his own results. He'd tried several positions at Peece Canning but had failed to stay interested. Inspired. The feeling that he was about to strike gold had everything to do with learning how to prune his cherry trees. It had nothing to do with a pair of milk chocolate–colored eyes framed by thick, dark lashes.

He turned off the main road and pulled into the driveway, parking near a big red truck with a plow. Eva's? If so, it was a mighty big vehicle for such a diminutive woman. He climbed out of his Jeep and breathed deeply. The February air seared his lungs, but he didn't care about the cold. He felt alive for the first time in a very long while.

Recommitting his heart to God at Christmas had been part of a series of changes he'd made in his life. Pushing thirty, it was about time he discovered his purpose. What God meant for him to do and who to be.

God, please be with me and help me get it right. I don't want this to be one more screwup.

Adam stared out over the eighty acres that now belonged to him with a sense of awe. The morning sun shrouded by thin clouds cast a pink glow against the bare orchard sloping in front of him. The gray waters of Lake Leelanau shone in the distance like a flat stone dusted with snow and ice. Beyond the far hills, Lake Michigan bled into a gray sky with the sandy face of South Fox Island breaking the color of the horizon. The view was spectacular and humbled his spirit. Could he make this work?

"Morning, Peece. You going to be warm enough?" Eva Marsh dressed head to toe in deer-colored canvas, stepped off the porch with a big basket over her arm. Was she planning an ice picnic?

He walked toward her. He'd skied in frozen temperatures all over the world. He didn't have to dress like a northern Michigan yokel to stay warm. "I dressed for outside work, if that's what you mean."

The guy that followed Eva could have been her twin, except that he stood about a foot taller than her. Also dressed in heavy canvas coveralls, he towered over both of them.

"This is my brother Ryan. He's helping out today. A couple of interns at the research center can join us later in the week if you decide not to stay," Eva said.

He'd given Eva an expense budget, but he wasn't ready to use it. It looked as if he'd have to prove to his pretty employee that he had every intention of staying on permanently. God willing.

Even so, Adam extended his hand to Ryan. "Nice to meet you."

"This your first time pruning, Adam?" Ryan didn't look much older than Eva.

"Yes." And he was going to enjoy every minute of it.

Ryan glanced at Eva and she gave him an I-told-you-so look. Either Eva had picked up on his excitement or she'd conveyed her city-boy-can't-do-real-work prejudice to her brother. Probably the latter.

"We've got fifteen acres of dormant sweet cherry trees to do. Another five acres of young sweets need pruning come spring. My dad had the tart orchard pruned last year so that'll be good for another couple years yet," Eva said over her shoulder.

Adam followed her as she strode toward a two-story barnlike garage with red clapboard siding that matched the house. With a push of a button, one of the two doors lifted with a squeak against the cold. Three ATVs were parked inside.

His pulse kicked up a few beats. "Nice."

"You like to ride?" Ryan asked.

"Anything with speed and I'm there." Adam kept pace with Ryan into the garage.

Ryan laughed, making clouds of white with his breath. "Me, too. My dad bought a third four-wheeler because Eva doesn't play passenger very well."

Adam glanced at Eva. He could see that.

Eva started the engine of her ATV, drove it into the driveway and stopped. A small wagon loaded with gear had been hooked onto the back. She pulled up her fleece balaclava to cover her nose and revved the engine. "Follow me, Peece."

"You seem to like my last name."

Eva's pretty eyes widened over the rim of her fleece covering. "I can call you sir if you'd rather."

He wondered why she wouldn't use his first name. "No way. Peece is fine, but it's what my college roommates called me. If I regress, that's on you."

A smile reached her eyes. "I'll take my chances."

Adam enjoyed this spunky Eva who looked ready for anything. He started his engine and, with a grin, squealed the tires out of the garage. In no time, they were jostling down a pristine white path into the orchard. They passed a section of smaller trees, their bases wrapped with what looked like plastic tubes. At one point, Ryan veered off into a parallel row and sped forward, spraying a tail of snow.

Adam grinned and followed suit. He couldn't get lost with only one way to go, straight ahead. So he gunned it.

He looked back to see Eva chugging behind them. Ryan tore down the next row over, so Adam bit the racing bait with a jerky jump forward as he revved the throttle. Playing chase, they sped along slipping between trees until Ryan darted in another direction. From out of nowhere, the path ended. The orchard stopped and a fence loomed ahead.

Adam swerved left. Applying the brake too quick, he spun and tipped into a cherry tree. His shoulder hit first, then the four-wheeler pinned his leg against a surprisingly solid mass for a thin trunk. Great. He was stuck. After a few minutes of trying and failing to loosen his leg enough to leverage the ATV back onto all four wheels, he heard Eva's approach.

She shook her head at him as if he'd been caught stealing one of her scones without asking. "What are you, twelve?"

So much for worrying about him. He wasn't physically hurt, just his pride, but still, she could at least *look* concerned. He laughed. "Sometimes."

He heard her chuckle under her breath, and then

she climbed up onto the high side foot bed and grabbed the handlebar. With considerable strength for her small stature and a deep grunt, she leaned back and righted his ATV.

He rubbed his calf. "Ow, that was my leg…"

"You're the one tearing around." She gave him a smarty-pants grin and then, without tossing an ounce of pity his way, she knelt and gently ran her gloved hands down the trunk of the tree he'd hit.

"Hey, what about me?"

She pulled down her balaclava. "You'll live. The tree might not."

He climbed off his four-wheeler and knelt next to her. "Why?"

She scooted around to the other side of the tree, looking for damage there. "See this gash?"

Instead of concentrating on her instruction, he watched her pretty face. The tip of her nose looked red. "Yeah."

Abruptly, she stood and stepped to the other side of the ATV. "Wound a tree and insects or rot can set in. Get a bad case of bugs because of a wound, and lose an entire section of crop."

"Oh."

"Yeah. Oh." She'd reduced him to feeling like a twelve-year-old. One who'd just been clued in to the serious consequences of his actions.

"Can't you put some goop on it, or wax?"

She shook her head. "Doesn't work that way.

Artificial remedies usually make it worse. I'll have Ryan check it out. It's a young tree. It might heal itself. We'll have to keep an eye on it come spring."

Adam liked the sound of her using the word *we*. He wanted them to work as a team. Despite being her boss, he wanted to establish a comfortable working relationship that was friendly. But not too friendly. Considering how attractive he found Eva, that might present a challenge.

"Come on, we'll trim a few rows down." Eva climbed back on her four-wheeler.

He followed at a sedate pace. In minutes they stopped and Eva grabbed a milk crate from the back of his ATV.

"What's that for?" Adam asked.

"Reaching the middle branches. I've got extended loppers for the tops."

She lugged a small stepladder from her wagon. "I need a little more height."

Adam laughed.

After getting set up, Eva motioned for him to come closer. "This is what we're trying to do. Look at the tree and envision it covered with leaves. Prune back branches that will block sunlight to the center of the tree. Light makes more cherries."

He recognized the same fire in Eva's eyes that had been in her father's. The same passion for the work. Robert Marsh had been right. No one cared more for this orchard than his daughter. Last fall, Adam had fallen in love with this land just as they had, only he needed to learn how to make it grow and produce a living.

She gestured for him to come near. "Watch how I make the cuts. We'll work down this row, then come back on the next one over."

Eva stood on the top step, so Adam took the bottom. Through the smell of ATV exhaust on her jacket, he caught a delicate scent. Maybe it was her perfume, or the shampoo she'd used. Whatever it was, he wouldn't mind getting a closer sniff. He peered around her shoulder, breathing deep. "Looks easy enough."

"Once you get the hang of it." She turned to look at him but leaned too far back and slipped.

"Whoa." Adam grabbed her upper arms to keep her from toppling.

She overcompensated and slipped down onto the bottom step, landing on his foot. Her eyes went wide and Adam caught a flicker of panic race across her face. "You can let go."

He stepped back and raised his hands in surrender. "I didn't want you to fall. Worker's comp is not good on the first day."

Adam smiled but he was curious to know what pulling her close would feel like. He suspected that she'd fit pretty well in his arms.

Eva inhaled big gulps of frosty air while her pulse

hammered in her ears. She needed to put space between her and Adam fast. Those bright blue eyes of his were a drowning place where she worried she couldn't stay afloat. "Thanks. Think you can handle your own set of loppers?"

He chuckled. "Absolutely."

"Good." But could she handle working beside Adam? She wasn't sure. It didn't really matter. She had a job to do, so she'd better toughen up real quick.

They pruned tree after tree with little conversation other than Eva checking his cuts and admitting he did them well. She'd catch Adam humming and then he'd smile at her, making her insides pitch.

She wished she didn't find Adam Peece so attractive. She might as well ask the sky to stop snowing for all the good it would do. *Why, God? Why'd it have to be someone so handsome like him?*

Although Eva attended church every week, she wasn't exactly on good speaking terms with the Lord. She stopped expecting His help a couple years ago after blaming God for what her boyfriend Todd had done. There was no easy way of getting over that kind of betrayal.

Eva made another vicious chop, but cutting off her memories wasn't as easy as trimming a cherry tree. Mistrust lurked deep in her still, ruining any hopes she'd had of dating. It was easier to keep guys at a safe distance. She stayed in control that way.

Eva blew out a breath of pent-up air. But then Adam Peece barged into her controlled world and lingered in her thoughts far too often. Working long hours beside him was bound to be more difficult than she anticipated.

What if she grew to care for him? Not likely, but working together for months in the field, who knew? Still, Eva wasn't cut out for a guy like Adam Peece. And someone like him wouldn't give her a serious look. Not in a thousand Sundays.

Shortly after noon, Ryan pulled up on his four-wheeler. "I'm hungry, Eva, what'd you bring to eat?"

"Stuff." She trudged toward her ATV, stepladder in hand. Her brother had eaten a huge breakfast before they came out, but it was tough keeping that six-foot-two frame of his filled. "Come on. I guess a break's in order. Bring your crate to sit on, Peece."

Adam had caught on to pruning quickly, making clean cuts and moving on. She'd checked his work repeatedly and was more than satisfied with what she saw. She didn't want him to enjoy this. She wished he'd go back to his canning kingdom in Detroit and let her do the work in peace. She'd make a good farm manager, but hands-on teacher? Right.

She opened her basket and drew out three thermoses. "Here's tomato soup."

"Come on, Eva, that won't fill me up," Ryan whined, perched on his four-wheeler.

"And chicken salad sandwiches." She offered one to Adam before handing the plate to her brother. "There's hot chocolate, too. Well, it's probably lukewarm by now."

"Cherries?" Adam looked up from his sandwich.

"She puts them in everything," Ryan said.

Eva made a face. "If you're going to complain, you can make your own lunch."

"I'm just stating a fact." Her brother laughed at her.

Eva knew she'd overreacted. Just because Adam got under her skin was no excuse to take it out on Ryan.

"How long will pruning take?" Adam blew into his gloves.

"On these trees? A few weeks." Eva smiled. If he skipped the rest of it, Eva might get more work done with Ryan's help and his two interns. Most of them knew how to trim a fruit tree as part of their agricultural education.

"That long?"

"Sometimes longer. Depends on the amount of help." Eva took a drink of warm soup.

"Your dad said he had two sons. Where's your other brother?" Adam sipped from his thermos.

Eva glanced at Ryan. "He's out on the mission field."

Her brother snorted. "Wasting time, if you ask me."

"Ryan!"

Adam looked confused. "He's a missionary?"

Eva nodded. "Sin's an ordained minister, but he's more into education. He's training native missionaries in Haiti."

Adam tipped his head. "Your brother's name is Sin?"

"Short for Sinclair."

"Ironic nickname for a minister."

Ryan laughed. "Not if you knew him."

"Just stop it." Eva bit into her sandwich. It hurt that her brothers hardly spoke. They were both hardheaded and sticking to what they thought were noble principles. Sinclair punished himself for his part in an accident that took the life of Ryan's girlfriend. Ryan blamed himself, but he resented Sin's absence. He'd had to face Sara's folks alone.

After lunch, Eva grabbed the long pruning loppers to tackle another row of trees. Within hours, the snowflakes grew fatter and more insistent. They stuck to her eyelashes and blurred her vision. She brushed them away.

She glanced at Adam on his milk crate. He'd slowed down considerably from this morning and kept blowing into his gloves. "Are you cold?"

"Just my hands."

She searched the wagon. Pulling out another pair of heavy-duty work gloves, she walked toward him. "Try these."

Adam tucked his expensive-looking ski gloves into his coat pockets. The tips of his fingers were white with a purple hue.

Eva grabbed his hands. "Let me see."

Adam tried to pull back. "They're fine."

"No, they're not." Eva took off her gloves and touched his frozen skin. "We have to get you back to the house."

"Give me those and I'll be fine."

"Nope. You've got frostbite starting on your fingertips. Time to call it a day. I'll let Ryan know." Eva looked at Adam's face. The tip of his nose had turned white, too. The most important thing was to get Adam back home where it was warm.

Adam sat in Eva's cheerfully decorated kitchen once again. Antiques mixed with brightly colored modern-looking fabrics but it blended well. The place had life. Vibrance. This time his hands were plunged into bowls of warm water while Eva built a fire in the woodstove. The snap and crackle of igniting wood cut the silence. And Adam felt like an idiot. Obviously he needed better gloves, and he'd have to pick up a fleece balaclava to protect his face if he planned to work an eight-hour day alongside the formidable Eva Marsh.

"So, I take it your family are churchgoers, to have a brother in ministry." Adam couldn't take the quiet. It was too much like when he was in grade school and sent to the principal's office.

"Yup."

"I went to church when I was a kid." His mother used to take him to Sunday school and church every week. A few years after she'd died, when he'd hit his teens, Adam took a detour away from everything he'd been taught about honoring God. He stayed on that road too long, making choices he wasn't proud of now that he'd given his heart back to the Lord.

Eva shut the woodstove doors. "Do you attend now?"

"When I can." He wanted to settle in somewhere and go regularly. He needed a home church to call his own. A place to grow.

After attending a Christian concert with his sister over the holidays, Adam hadn't anticipated God grabbing hold of him, but he was grateful for the second chance. Another puzzle piece of his life found its place. Adam might not have all the pieces locked in yet, but he was on his way.

He looked her square in the eye and wanted her to know he'd changed. "I recently came back to my faith."

Her eyes widened with surprise. "Looks like you'll have to change your lifestyle."

She couldn't know what his life had been before—the parties filled with women and friends looking for what they could glean from him. Not that he cared to enlighten her. He was over it. Finished. Still, he smiled at her sharp tongue, and then laughed when the shock on her face registered as if she'd accidentally spoken her thoughts out loud.

Adam knew he had a lot to live down. "I thought Christians were supposed be nice. Love thy neighbor and pray for your enemies."

Her eyes glazed with remorse, and then she laughed, but her amusement sounded forced. "Yeah, well, I'm working on that."

"So, have you decided if I'm your neighbor or your enemy?"

She glanced at the clock on the wall, obviously uncomfortable with his probing. "I don't know yet."

But the brief flash of pain in her chocolatey eyes bothered him. It wasn't easy accepting his part in her disappointment. He knew buying her family's orchard had been a blow to her dreams of one day taking over the farm. Her father had pretty much spelled that out.

But Adam suspected the resentment went deeper than the sale of the land. She seemed lost and alone. Almost afraid, like a small force in a big world gone awry. Which was crazy considering that Eva Marsh proved quite capable of taking care of herself.

"Let me see your hands." Eva peeked into the bowl, effectively shutting down his thoughts by her nearness. Something about her definitely piqued his interest.

He lifted his hands and winced.

She glanced at him with real concern and then gently touched the skin of his fingers. "As they thaw, it's going to hurt."

"You're not kidding." Adam had experienced cold but never like this. He peered into Eva's eyes, and for a few moments she didn't look away. She didn't let go of his hands either.

And then the door opened, and Eva's roommate blew in with a rush of bitter air. Beth took one look at him and rushed forward. "Adam, what happened?"

"Frostbite." Eva moved away, leaving Adam to wish her roommate back at school.

Beth's expression turned to mush. "Oh, you poor thing. Can I get you anything?"

This was what Adam was used to, but oddly enough he didn't want Beth hovering over him. "I'll be fine."

She smiled. "You gotta watch Eva, she's a tough taskmaster."

Adam noticed the flush of color on Eva's cheeks and grinned. "She's not so bad."

"Wait till you get to know her better." Beth winked at him.

Had Eva heard Beth's comment? By the way his prickly little employee bustled about the kitchen, he was pretty sure she had. Maybe she wasn't immune to him after all.

After the first week's worth of pruning beside Adam, Eva needed to unwind. Saturday night, she succeeded for a couple of hours at the movies with Ryan and Beth. She hadn't thought of Adam Peece once during the big-budget sci-fi flick. Except for the moment she decided that the lead actor's brilliant blue eyes were no comparison to Adam's.

After his bout with frostbite, Adam had shown up for work wearing better gear and he went the distance in the field. She thought for sure he'd bail after a few days spent working outside in the bitter cold. Instead, he arrived every morning eager to work. Ryan had shown him how to use a small chainsaw on the bigger branches needing to be clipped from older trees.

The instant camaraderie between the two men pricked like a thorn in her finger. She'd always considered her brother a good judge of character. Either his discernment was off or her apprehension of Adam was overblown. Neither sat well.

"Wanna grab a bite to eat?" Ryan pulled his truck into the latest hot spot in Traverse City.

"Why here?" Eva didn't care to hang out in a loud place.

"They have the best wings in town. Come on, Beth, back me up."

Beth laughed. "You're looking to scope the ladies."

"Right." Ryan's mouth twisted.

Eva had given up badgering Ryan to ask Beth out since her brother showed no signs of interest. For anyone. His hurt still ran too deep. But then, so did hers.

After they found a table, Eva looked around the crowded restaurant. The bar was full, and the surrounding tables were jammed. She spotted movement in the corner and heard shrill feminine laughter. And then she saw him.

Adam sat at the end of a table made for eight with at least twelve people squeezed around it. Adam sat between two women, his arms draped loosely around each one.

"Hey, Adam." Ryan waved.

Under the table, Eva pinched her brother's thigh. "Don't call him over here."

"Why not?" Ryan feigned innocence.

Beth turned and waved, too.

It was hard enough working with him—Eva didn't want to socialize, too. But like a fly drawn to rotting fruit, Eva glanced at Adam. His blue eyes stared straight through her as he disengaged from the pouty-lipped women and made his way toward them.

"Great," Eva growled.

"How come your cheeks are red, Eva?" Ryan winked.

She wanted to hide, which made her cheeks feel that much hotter.

Beth played traitor and pulled out a chair.

Adam slipped into the seat. "Had some great skiing today. What are you guys up to?"

"We went to the movies," Beth answered.

Eva peeked at the table Adam had left behind. Some of the women took pictures with their cell phones. Maybe that was why he'd been cuddled between two beauties—he was getting his picture taken. Not that it was any of her business what he did.

"Are you guys interested in coming to my place to ski tomorrow? I'll spring for your lift tickets."

"Cool."

"No, thanks," Eva answered with more volume than her brother. "We've got church in the morning."

Ryan looked at her as if she'd spit ice cubes across the table and then turned to Adam. "Why don't you come with us to church? We can ski afterward."

Eva jumped in before Adam could answer. "He's not going to want to drive all the way from Benzie County for church."

"Let the man answer for himself," Ryan said.

Eva glanced at Adam. He fiddled with the salt and pepper shakers, but his gaze rested firmly on her. The taunt she'd flung at him about changing his lifestyle rang through her brain. Surely he wouldn't attend church to spite her.

"Hmm. I'm staying at a friend's place not too far from you guys, so I could make church."

Eva cringed. Ryan had a big mouth.

"I'd love to ski, but I have dinner plans with my mom right after service. Why don't you pick us up at nine thirty?" Beth's smile was a little too wide.

Adam tapped the table with his fingertips. Not a trace of damage from his scrape with frostbite. "Is that okay with you, Eva?"

What could she say? Refusing now would only make her look like being around Adam got to her. Backed into a corner, she decided nonchalance was the best shield of defense. "Sure, that's fine."

He studied her longer than she thought necessary before answering. "Then I'll see you tomorrow morning."

Eva watched him return to his table of *friends*. The volume of laughter rose, and one of the women he'd had his arm around threw her a curious glance and then settled on Beth. Creases of doubt wrinkled the woman's forehead.

Ryan rubbed his chin. "I'm definitely taking him up on his offer to ski tomorrow. You going, Eva?"

"No!" Maybe she'd been abrupt in her answer, but the company Adam Peece kept supported what she thought. He was a shallow guy trying out a new hobby. Those women at his table no doubt thought a gentleman cherry grower was a charming side job. Eva might work for the man, but she wasn't about to hang out with him, too. No way, no how.

Chapter Three

The next morning, Adam knocked on Eva's door wondering if he'd made a wise choice. It was the perfect day to ski, blue skies filled with sunshine and temperatures topping out at a balmy thirty degrees. He had the strangest sense that he'd feel closer to God on the slopes rather than sitting in a pew next to Miss Prickly Prim Marsh.

Beth opened the door. "Good morning, Adam. Come in. Eva will be down in a minute. Want some coffee?"

Adam stepped into the warm kitchen and shed his coat. "I'd love some."

Beth handed him a mug of steaming brew. "Have you had breakfast? It'd only take a minute to warm up Eva's oatmeal."

Adam nestled on a stool, propping his elbows on the ceramic tile-covered island while he cradled his cup. "I'm not much of a hot cereal fan."

"I promise you'll like this. If not, no big deal." Beth shrugged, but Adam got the distinct feeling that if he didn't like it there was something wrong with him.

Maybe there was more than just the cereal at stake here, Adam mused. He suspected that if he messed with Eva, he'd have to answer to her roommate. A tall, solid-looking woman, Beth was a formidable force. "I'll give it a try."

Beth smiled. "You won't be sorry."

They were talking about the cereal, right?

He shook off his musings. Something about the brown sugar and spice smell of Eva's kitchen felt like home. A real home. Not the rambling, fully staffed estate of his father's where Adam and his siblings each had private apartments.

Adam stirred milk into his bowl of oatmeal that was loaded with nuts and berries. "She puts cherries in everything, doesn't she?"

"Just about. She loves them. She loves this orchard, too, if you haven't already noticed."

Adam didn't miss the serious note in Beth's voice. He remembered the way Eva fussed over the young tree he'd gashed with the ATV and felt like a heel all over again. "That's why I hired her."

Beth quickly turned to put away the remains of breakfast. Though he couldn't guess why, Beth seemed disappointed with his answer.

Adam took a bite of cereal, savoring the heat and texture. "Wow. This is good."

"Thanks." Eva entered the room dressed in a butter-colored sweater and matching pants that hugged her slender form. Her hair gleamed against her shoulders and her lips had been slicked with berry-tinted gloss.

Adam dropped his spoon. He glanced at Beth, who smiled at him again, only this time with beaming approval. She'd witnessed his jaw-drop reaction to seeing Eva dressed like a girl instead of a farmhand. And he could practically hear the matchmaking gears turning inside Beth's head.

Adam focused on his breakfast. He had no business finding Eva Marsh so attractive. Any entanglement with her would throw a wrench in what he was trying to figure out. Trying to do.

He'd done more than his fair share of dating. He needed to stay away from that slippery slope. Besides, he'd never get tangled up with an employee. Unlike his father, who had a habit of getting involved with his secretaries, Adam kept work and his personal life separated.

He peeked at Eva leaning against the counter. She watched him over the rim of her coffee cup. Attending church with her inched pretty close to that personal line.

Eva didn't like the hitch in her breathing when she read the appreciation in Adam's eyes. She didn't like admitting that she'd taken extra care getting dressed this morning either. But that was exactly what she'd done, all because she was trying to compete with the beauties at Adam's table last night. Ridiculous, considering she'd never come close by comparison. She shouldn't care. Eva knew who she was and where she came from.

Still, she hadn't been prepared for his approval or searching curiosity when he'd stared at her. She took too big a gulp of coffee. Swallowing the heat brought tears to her eyes and she coughed.

"You okay?" Beth asked.

"Coffee too hot."

Adam brought his bowl to the sink, putting him much too close for comfort. "You going to make it?"

Eva coughed again.

He touched her elbow. "You okay?"

She stepped away. "Thanks, I'm fine. Really. Let's go."

But she wasn't fine. For a split second, Eva had wanted to sway closer to Adam. Like a magnet drawn to steel, she'd felt a sharp pull between them. She didn't need to act on it. She wouldn't.

"Eva, you coming?" Beth slipped into her coat.

"Yes." She brushed her thoughts aside and grabbed her jacket.

Could men like Adam Peece be trusted? Not by her. No matter how nice he seemed, Peece was used to getting what he wanted when he wanted it. Despite having to work with him, Eva would keep her distance. Despite friendly outings to church, Eva was his employee. There was no point in dressing to catch his attention. She shouldn't want it.

But she did.

The small church was full of people chatting in the foyer when they arrived and Adam felt the weight of several stares. Both men and women scrutinized him closely. He didn't fit the flannel shirt and blue jeans dress code of a northern Michigan small town. So what if his clothes screamed out-of-towner? He liked to look nice.

Eva was pulled aside by a little old lady with blue hair. The elderly woman whispered in Eva's ear and made her laugh out loud. Adam realized he'd never heard Eva really laugh. He liked it.

"Adam, this is my grandma Marsh." Eva's eyes were shining with amusement.

Adam looked at the woman, who was not much taller than Eva but with the same chocolate-brown eyes that proved a family resemblance. He took the lady's hand in his own. "Very nice to meet you."

Grandma squeezed his fingers with surprising strength. "My, my, but you're a looker. I've got my eye on you, young man."

Adam swallowed a laugh and winked at her instead. "I hope so."

He glanced at Eva, who shook her head before saying, "I'm going to get Grandma settled next to Aunt Jamee and Uncle Larry."

"I'll catch up with you in the sanctuary." He watched them walk away.

"So, what do you think?" Beth asked him.

Adam turned to see Beth looking smug. "Of what?"

"Of Eva."

Adam didn't understand why her roommate kept tossing Eva at him as if she was incapable of attracting a guy on her own. That was a new one. He was used to pushy girls like Beth hoping to snatch him for themselves, not their friends. He wasn't interested in romancing Eva. He shouldn't be. "Ah… yeah…well, she's capable. Why do you keep asking me?"

Beth shrugged her shoulders, but she gave him that satisfied grin that only girls could muster. The one that said she'd gotten the answer she was looking for even though he hadn't said a thing. "No reason."

He rolled his eyes when she walked away. Maybe he should find an excuse to leave early. But then Ryan made a beeline for him with an intense-looking man pushing fifty.

"Hey," Adam said.

"Adam, I want to introduce you to my uncle. He's been our beekeeper for as long as I can remember, but Eva can fill you in on details. Uncle Larry, this is Adam Peece. He bought the orchard from Dad."

"Peece? Any relation to the canning company?" Larry extended his hand.

"My father's business, third-generation owner."

The man gave him a shrewd look. "As the fourth generation, are you looking to move into cherries now?"

Adam saw where this was going. He wanted to set Larry straight. "No, I decided to go it alone. Although, if my dad wants to buy them from me come harvest, I won't complain."

Larry slapped him on the back, satisfied with the answer. "Absolutely not. Come on, I'll introduce you to a grower that also rents bees from me. He's a good man to know around here."

Adam gave Ryan a nod and went with his uncle. Larry introduced him to Jim Sandborn, a cherry and apple farmer who lived about five miles south of Marsh Orchards.

"New to fruit farming then?" Jim eyed him with apprehension.

Last year, Adam had come to Leelanau County to investigate buying fruit from the area processors. He'd made no secret of researching the particulars for a new product line he wanted to propose to his father.

Adam met Robert Marsh at one such processor

and after a long conversation Adam toured the man's property. That first glimpse of Marsh Orchards had been like hearing a siren's song that dug deep into his blood and stayed there. The more he listened to Eva's father talk about growing cherries, the more Adam wanted to experience it. The more Adam saw of the land, the more he wanted to own it.

"I'm brand-new. But I've hired Eva Marsh as my manager to show me the ropes."

The hardened farmer with hair whiter than the snow piled up outside cracked a hint of a smile. "Lots of you young fellers trying yer hand at cherry farming. But Eva's a smart girl, that one. Known her since she was knee-high. Tiny but just like her dad, and stubborn, too. Let me know if you need anything."

"Thanks. I will." Adam hoped the guy meant what he'd said. Admitting that he worked with Eva was what had melted Jim's frosty stare. He wondered if the other growers might relax as quickly once they knew Eva was his manager.

The music started and Adam extended his hand. "Nice to meet you, Jim."

The man shook it, nodded and wandered into church.

Adam followed suit, surprised to see Eva waiting for him.

"We sit near the front." Her eyes challenged him.

He wasn't about to back away, even if they'd been in the very first row. "Closer to the action. I like that."

He slid into the fourth-row pew right before Ryan could slip in. Adam sat beside Eva. He grinned at the annoyed look she flashed him before she scooted as far away from him as the large lady seated on the other side allowed. He couldn't help but chuckle at her prickly reaction.

The service started with singing, and the congregation didn't hold back in volume or enthusiasm. Adam glanced around. Most of the church members looked like farmers or typical small-town stock. He spotted Uncle Larry sitting between an attractive woman who had to be Aunt Jamee and Grandma Marsh. Larry nodded in acknowledgment.

Adam faced the front and clapped along. He liked the feel of this church with its warm, open faces. By the time the minister stood at the podium, memories of attending services like this with his mom flooded his thoughts. Coming to church had been a good call, even though Eva's proximity distracted. He was aware of her every move.

Eva tried to concentrate on the service, but it was impossible with Adam next to her. From the deep tone of his singing voice pleasantly tickling her ears, to the sincerity of his whispered prayers, she was undone.

Incredible! Adam Peece was a real man of faith.

He hadn't been kidding. The knowledge didn't mix well with the image of Adam with his group of friends last night. Not that any of them did anything wrong, but it was hard to reconcile those two sides of her boss. He was the life of the party but quietly serious in worship.

Watching him with his eyes closed pierced her spirit with an ache of longing. She missed the close relationship she used to have with the Lord. Eva had kept prayer journals during her daily devotions, but she hadn't opened one in two years.

A gnawing in the pit of her stomach hinted that maybe it was time to stop blaming God for what had happened to her. She'd held on so long to the Lord's lack of protection, when she needed to accept that she'd made a horrible mistake trusting Todd. Her mistake. One she'd never make again.

Once the service concluded, she inched her way out of the crowded row, sensing Adam right behind her. The warmth of his nearness surrounded her even though he remained a proper few inches away. She stopped to wait for a woman to gather up a diaper bag.

"Hey, Eva." Beth appeared from behind two elderly ladies. "Ryan's dropping me off at my mom's. I'll see you later tonight."

Eva nodded. Great. That left Adam to drive her home alone.

"I see an opening." Adam took her by the hand. "Come on, we better make a break for it."

Eva noticed that Adam's touch was warm, although his palm felt rougher than she expected from a paper-pusher. Careful to watch that she didn't bump into anyone, she followed Adam's weaving between groups of people.

An expanse of solid man stood in her way, then he spoke. "Hello, Eva."

She stopped short at the sound of that terrible voice. The voice she hadn't heard in two years. The voice belonging to a man she'd thought she loved until he'd attacked her.

Todd!

The last time she'd heard Todd's voice he'd bellowed drunken obscenities when Beth had helped her get away from him.

Her hand slipped out of Adam's grasp as the clamoring buzz in her ears drowned out the sounds and faces of the people surrounding her. Todd blocked out the light of her tunnel vision, making her feel dizzy. Sick.

She sucked in air, but it didn't help. Stars formed before her eyes. She was going to faint. Right there. In the middle of the sanctuary, she'd fall. Adam would see and he'd know. He'd tell Ryan. And Ryan would go after Todd.

No!

Stepping back until her bottom connected with a

pew, Eva gripped the solid wood until she felt a fingernail crack. The pain helped her focus, helped her calm down a shade. She tried to make her mouth work, but nothing came out despite hearing herself scream on the inside.

"It's been a while."

"Yes," she croaked.

"This is my wife, Susan. We're up from Grand Rapids visiting my in-laws who attend here."

Eva's eyes widened when she took in the pretty woman standing next to him with a pink bundle of baby in her arms.

The woman's eyes narrowed as if recognizing her. But they'd never met. "Nice to meet you."

She felt the warmth of Adam's hand at the small of her back.

"Everything okay?" Adam's voice sounded far away, as if he was talking from the other side of a long tunnel.

"I—" Eva looked back at Todd. The urge to yell and pound on him overwhelmed her, sapping her strength. He acted as if nothing out of the ordinary had ever passed between them.

"Todd, honey, we better go. Dad's pulled the car up front." Susan shifted her pink burden and moved toward the door.

"Look, Eva…" He reached out a hand but let it drop with a sigh. He gave her an awkward smile and then nodded toward Adam. "Take it easy, okay?"

Eva didn't know if she responded. Her knees shook, and her stomach lurched. Sweat broke out along her hairline. She really was going to be sick.

Why here? Why now?

"Eva?" Adam touched her elbow.

She shrank away from him.

"Who is that guy? Did he say something to upset you?"

Eva closed her eyes with a quick shake of her head. Seeing Todd upset her. Seeing him happily married and blessed with a beautiful baby girl infuriated her. How could God be so cruel? Todd had flourished, while Eva was stuck in a hellish purgatory she couldn't climb out of.

She felt the gentle pressure of Adam's hand return to the small of her back. "Come on. I'll take you home."

Adam drove with the heat cranked to full blast. He kept glancing at Eva huddled in her seat. She hadn't quit shivering. He wanted to pull over and gather her into his arms, but he didn't trust the wildness in her gaze. The fury. He feared he might make matters worse by offering unwanted comfort.

"You okay?"

She nodded.

"Old boyfriend?"

She glanced at him with haunted eyes. "Yeah."

The ex-boyfriend was a giant of a man who looked far too clumsy for a petite thing like Eva. He struck Adam as one of those unmotivated types with boring stability stamped across his forehead. Eva needed someone who'd keep up with and challenge her. Maybe she had bossed the big dude around too much. Maybe that was why he'd left her. "Want to talk about it?"

"No."

Adam glanced her way again and she looked close to tears. He gripped the steering wheel tighter. Tears weren't good. A snappy Eva he understood, but a sad Eva busted him up. "It's okay to unload."

"I don't want to unload. Why don't *you* unload? What are you doing here, Peece?"

He braced himself for the unleashing of that pent-up anger. "What do you mean?"

"You're the green bean heir. Why'd you buy my cherry orchard? To play nice and sweet so you could get in good with the growers to rip them off some-how? A guy like you can't be serious about working a farm. Do you really think you belong here?"

Adam knew why he was here, but Eva wouldn't believe him if he explained the calling that had filled him the day he saw the orchard. Maybe it was part of how God had whispered through the branches to woo him back into the fold like a sheep gone lost. Adam didn't know.

All he knew was that he *had* to have the land.

It was bigger than his grandfather's farm, but it beckoned with the same promise of a simpler, better life. Away from his past where so-called friends looked at him with greed-filled eyes. And women wanted him more for what he could do for them financially.

Adam desperately needed a simpler life.

Explaining the whys would be a waste of breath. Eva struck him as a person who needed action, not words. Proof. Besides, she was hurting. Bad. If she wanted to take it out on him, he could handle it.

He pulled into her driveway but didn't shut off the engine. The hum of the heater pouring out warm air masked the silence. Adam turned toward her. He didn't want her to bolt, not yet. "What if I do belong here?"

She stared at him with her sweet mouth hanging open, looking as if the world around her had crumbled. "I miss the way things were."

He gently touched her shoulder, wishing he could ease whatever it was that tore her up. Wishing he could promise her that she'd never get hurt again, but that was not the way life worked. "I'm sorry."

Just then, Ryan's truck pulled in next to them and the moment was lost. Eva exited the car and made for the house quicker than a jackrabbit.

Adam shut off the engine and got out.

"What's wrong with Eva?" Ryan wore the concerned look of a brother ready to defend his sister if needed.

"She's upset about some guy who showed up at church."

Ryan's eyes narrowed, as if weighing the truth.

Adam couldn't blame him. He'd be concerned, too, if it were his sister. He looked up into Ryan's gaze without flinching.

Finally, Ryan slapped him on the back. "Come on, man. Eva's bound to have something good for lunch and we can talk her into going skiing. She doesn't get out much, and it sounds like she needs an afternoon of fun."

Eva wouldn't look at Adam throughout the meal. His eyes had a way of luring her in and keeping her. She had to prove that she could do this job. Mouthing off like that to her boss was a good way to get fired. Instead, Adam had understood and even attempted to comfort her. And he wanted her to go skiing.

That might be the best way to get back in his good graces after such an awful display of emotion. She couldn't stay home alone. Not now, not after seeing Todd. This morning had taken its toll, dredging up all the fury and fear she still wrestled with.

Maybe skiing would end up being therapeutic. She hadn't skied in years, but it was better than staying alone until Beth returned. She'd ride with her brother, and that should give her a reprieve from dodging questions laced with good intentions.

On the way, she realized how wrong her reasoning had been when Ryan asked, "So what's up with you two?"

She stared out the passenger window of his truck. "What are you talking about?"

"I have eyes. You were crying when you got out of Adam's car."

Eva gritted her teeth. She'd lost it, but she'd recovered in time to fix lunch. She didn't think Ryan had noticed. "Todd was in church. He's married with a baby girl."

"Why'd you two break up anyway?" Ryan followed behind Adam's fancy four-door Jeep Wrangler.

It was the kind of vehicle that suited Adam. The doors, the hard top and who knew what else could be taken off. Adam loved zipping around on the ATVs, so she imagined he'd love to go two-tracking, as well. Unless he never got that Jeep dirty. Unless it was all for show from a city boy who liked the idea of having a fun car but didn't put it to use.

Eva turned her attention back to Ryan and shrugged. No one knew about Todd, only Beth. "Because he's a jerk."

"Then you're better off without him. But why the tears after all this time?"

"I don't know." But she knew. She hadn't faced Todd since that night at a party two years ago. She'd never gone to the police because she couldn't drag her family through more junk after the death of Ryan's girlfriend.

Instead, Eva hoped she'd get over it. Fat chance. Seeing Todd brought back the pain almost as if it had happened last night.

"What do you think of Adam?"

Eva stared at the snow-covered landscape whizzing by. "I try not to."

Ryan laughed. "You like him, don't you?"

"No." Only partly true. She was afraid to like him.

"Come on, Eva. He's a good-looking guy with a fat wallet."

Eva closed her eyes. "So?"

"So, you haven't dated since you broke up with Todd."

"I've been on a few." Eva had gone on three dates, but they didn't work out. Her fault, not theirs.

"Maybe it's time you went on a few more."

"You're one to talk," Eva blurted.

Ryan's neck reddened. "I have my reasons."

Remorse pulled Eva into the melancholy place she frequented far too often. "Yeah, well, so do I."

After a few moments of silence, Eva felt Ryan looking at her. "What?"

"With Mom and Dad in Florida and Sin gone, it's up to me to look out for you. You're the youngest."

Her heart swelled into her throat, making it hard to swallow. "Thanks, brother dear, but I'm a big girl now. I can fend for myself."

"I know you can. But I'm here just the same."

"Thanks." Her eyes stung in the corners. Ryan was a good man, and he deserved better than what he'd been through. Bolstering her courage she asked, "Why didn't you move away after Sara died?"

"This is where Sara wanted to be. I won't ever leave."

Eva nodded, but her heart ached for her brother who'd lost the love of his life. Maybe that was why she and Ryan understood each other. They each accepted what they'd lost.

But Eva didn't want to accept losing her family's orchard. She'd do her best to show Adam the ropes even though she prayed for two things—he'd keep her on as farm manager long enough for her to get that loan and he wouldn't ruin the farm.

She needed those cherry orchard views to lure guests for her bed-and-breakfast.

Chapter Four

Ryan pulled in behind Adam's Jeep parked in the last driveway at the end of a row of large but unpretentious-looking town houses. Eva changed into her ski boots and then slipped out of her brother's truck to look around. Adam's place was tucked into the woods at the base of a hill. A stream wound its way through the complex that bespoke quiet living.

"Nice." Ryan gave a low whistle. "This guy has some cash."

"It belongs to his family." Pampered. That was what came to Eva's mind. Ski slopes and beach resorts were no doubt Peece family destinations. It was no wonder he could buy Marsh Orchards and give her folks the means to retire early.

Feeling out of place, Eva scanned the snowy trails that led toward the ski resort. Why'd she come? The question rang through her brain again when Ryan handed her the skis she last used as a teenager.

Hoisting them onto her shoulder, Eva wasn't sure joining Adam and Ryan had been such a good idea.

"You okay?" Adam had quickly changed into a trendy black ski jacket with matching black-and-red checked pants.

She shook herself out of her daze. "It's been a long time since I've done this."

"We can hit the easy trails first."

Eva glanced at her brother, who looked anxious to bomb the black diamond trails. How'd she turn out to be the only kid who played it safe in her family? "I don't want to hold you guys back. You two go on ahead. I can putter until I get my ski legs."

Adam handed Ryan a lift ticket, then turned to her with a grin. "There are some nice, gentle slopes here. And I'll give you some pointers. You'll do fine."

Great. Peece wasn't going to be easy to shake loose. She'd been hoping for a little solitude. Time to deal with seeing Todd.

"Trust me, you'll enjoy this." Adam grinned.

"Right." Adam had the kind of smile that made her want to believe everything he told her. Not good. She'd believed in Todd once.

"Come on, the lifts aren't far from here." Adam carried his skis tucked under his arm and led the way.

Ryan walked fast with antsy anticipation. It was

all Eva could do to keep up. When they made it to the base of the hill, Eva fiddled with her ancient bindings. If she took too long, maybe they'd go on without her.

"Need help?" Adam asked.

"I got it." Eva finally clicked in.

"Ready?" Adam asked.

"Absolutely." Ryan pushed forward.

Eva waddled close enough to pull on her brother's sleeve.

"What?"

"Don't ditch me," she whispered.

Ryan looked at her with a blank stare. "Why?"

She didn't want to get stuck with Adam, alone. She still felt raw, vulnerable. "Stay close."

He rolled his eyes. "You'll be fine, Eva."

At the main chairlift, Eva looked up and really wished she hadn't agreed to come. The trails looked steep.

Adam pulled another lift ticket out of his pocket. He slid close and handed it to her. "I know you can do this."

How could he know? She tried to force the clip onto her jacket's zipper, but her mittens made her movements clumsy. "I need easy, remember?"

"Don't worry. You'll ace the green trails in no time."

Eva noticed that Adam's right ski was practically on top of her left. She'd back up but didn't dare move for fear she'd slip and bring them both down into a heap. His leg brushed hers as he leaned toward her, sending a shiver down her spine that had nothing to do with the cold.

If Ryan left her, she'd kill him. She looked at Adam. "What are you doing?"

He grabbed the lift ticket from her fumbling mittened hands and clipped it onto her jacket with a quick snap. "You were bending it."

She let out the breath she'd been holding. "Oh."

His eyes searched hers. "Relax. This is supposed to be fun."

She nodded, but really, how could she relax? Her rich and handsome employer was inches from her face. She could smell his cologne. Nice, woodsy, expensive. Another jolt of awareness raced up her spine. There was no way she'd relax around Adam Peece.

"Let's go." Eva breathed.

Adam moved away from her with athletic grace. Turning easily on his skis, he led the way.

Eva jerked along, almost losing her balance twice.

On the chairlift, Eva was wedged between Adam and her brother. She checked out the view of vast rolling hills of white dotted with evergreens and naked brown hardwoods. And then she scanned the slope. This was a beautiful place filled with beautiful people. Adam included. He definitely belonged here. Several women checked him out with interest. Even with her sitting next to him.

But then, it must be obvious that they didn't go together. Adam wore expensive top-of-the-line ski attire and Eva had donned an old pink ski suit complete with a white patch on one elbow. Like a stale marshmallow Peep left over from an Easter basket, she was definitely out of date.

"When we get off, be sure to veer to the right. Then wait. There are a couple trailheads for this lift. I want to take the right one," Adam said.

Getting on a chairlift was one thing, getting off—completely different. The closer the crest loomed, the more the lift creaked, its gears pulling them closer to the launching pad. Eva's palms felt sweaty inside her mittens. She took a deep breath. "Okay."

"Eva, hand me your poles. Ryan, we'd better help her out."

Adam took her poles and then her hand. "Ready, step off and veer right. *Now.*"

Eva did as instructed. She wobbled, but between Adam's strong hand and Ryan's arm looped through hers, she steadied in the nick of time. They paused at the top of the main hill. The view stretched forever with rolling hills and pristine snow dotted with occasional homes peeking out from the forest.

She let out her breath with a whoop of relief. "That went well."

Adam grinned. "See? Nothing to it."

Eva laughed, but it sounded more like a strangled giggle. Her nerves were shot and she hadn't even started down the hill.

"I'll meet you guys at the bottom." Ryan slipped ahead of them and whooshed away.

"But—" Eva closed her mouth. If she expected to work alone with Adam for a full season, she had better get used to it sooner than later. Ryan wasn't available to play chaperone every day.

Adam handed over her poles. "Go ahead of me so I can watch your form."

Eva looked up sharply. "What's that?"

"Show me how you ski."

She pushed off, hoping she didn't look like a klutz. After a short span of shushing down the gentle slope, Adam passed her and then stopped in front of her with a spray of white snow.

Showoff was the first thought that came to mind. Instead she asked, "Well? What do you think?"

"You don't give yourself enough credit."

She warmed to the compliment. "What do you mean?"

"You're too stiff. Relax, lean forward and enjoy the ride."

"Lean forward? I thought I was supposed to bend my knees and lean back." Eva remembered those long-ago ski lessons her parents made her take.

Adam moved behind her. He slid one of his skis between her two and settled his hands lightly onto her shoulders. "Lean into the forward motion, and keep your head aligned with or over your feet."

Her spine immediately stiffened. That was enough of this lesson! She pushed forward too hard, slipped and fell.

Adam laughed, but he held out his hand. "Are you all right?"

Clenching her teeth, she gave him her hand. "Warn me next time you do that."

Again he laughed as he pulled her up. "Sorry. I'm used to hands-on lessons when showing someone how to ski better."

"What kind of ski lessons did you take?" She could only imagine. Eva leaned on her poles to catch her breath.

"Contrary to what you might have been taught, the key to flexibility and control is in your neck. Keep your head forward, breathe in deeply to expand your chest and relax your neck. The rest of your body will align."

She narrowed her eyes. Was he giving her a line?

"Watch me." He sailed effortlessly past her, then stopped and waited. "Give it a try."

She pushed off and zoomed forward, trying out what he'd told her. She wasn't sure if it worked, but it felt better. Adam had been on the up-and-up with his lesson. How paranoid of her to think otherwise.

"Great. You look great. Ready to take the hill?" Adam asked when she reached him.

"As ready as I'll ever be." Eva had come to ski. She couldn't get out of it, so she might as well get into it.

At least it kept her mind occupied. She'd have obsessed at home seeing the image of Todd with a wife and beautiful, blond-haired baby girl. Eva wanted her own babies one day, but how long would it take before she could enjoy a date? At the rate she was going, marriage might as well be Never Never Land.

She glanced at Adam sailing down the gentle trail ahead of her with surprising speed. Maybe working with a guy like him might actually help her. The looks he'd received from women of various ages reiterated that Adam could have his pick when it came to ladies. There was no way he'd take an interest in her. All she had to do was take comfort in that knowledge and learn how to relax around him. And maybe, just maybe, she'd learn how to put what happened with Todd behind her and move on.

Adam enjoyed showing Eva techniques to give her more confidence on the slopes. It was fun watching her work out her stance until she'd mastered keeping her head forward. If one thing could be said about Eva Marsh, it was that she didn't give up. Her brother teased her the entire time, but eventually, after several runs, even he complimented her skill.

Eager for speed and a challenge, Adam and Ryan broke away from Eva, leaving her content with staying on the easy green trails. Adam believed she was ready to tackle more difficult runs, but he wasn't going to push her. Eva might be a decent skier, but she still hesitated whenever she came upon a bunched-up crowd.

After a couple hours of hitting black diamond trails, Adam waited in the main chairlift line. He spotted a pink ski suit swishing toward them. He waved. "Eva!"

She looked up.

"Come with us. We can do a blue run."

Eva shook her head. "You guys go ahead."

"Come on, Eva," Ryan said. "You can do it."

Eva glanced at Adam.

"You're ready for them."

He watched her wrestle with the decision, until she finally gave in. "Okay, but I'm not going fast."

"Thatta girl." Ryan slapped his sister on the back, almost knocking her over.

Her pink fleece hat slipped forward, covering her eyes. She looked adorable in that awful ski suit.

The three of them took the main lift, settling into the same chair. This time, Eva aced her dismount and arched like a gymnast who'd nailed her landing. She laughed and then looked embarrassed as if she'd forgotten he was there. Her performance had been for her brother's benefit.

Ryan palmed his sister's shoulder and gave her a teasing shove. "Good job."

Eva laughed again, and Adam relished the sound. He admired the way Eva tackled whatever intimidated her. "Ready?"

"Let's see if she can keep up," her brother challenged.

Eva's brow furrowed. "Forget it, Ryan. I'm not racing."

"We'll meet you at the bottom," Adam told Ryan. He'd had his fill of speeding down runs. He waited for Eva, watching her brother tear down the trail until he was out of sight.

She waved him on. "Go ahead. I'm going to take my time on this one and get the feel of it."

He didn't mind going slow to ski beside her, but the glint in her eyes told him she'd rather do this on her own. Alone.

"I'll wait at the bottom then." He pushed off.

Loving the warmth of the February sun shining on his face, Adam leaned low and picked up speed. In no time, he passed Ryan.

At the bottom, he cut to a stop and turned to watch Ryan, who wasn't far behind. The guy bombed the hill with about as much grace as a farm tractor. Adam scanned the hill for a pink ski suit. Eva made her way at a decent pace. More cautious than her brother's reckless abandon, Eva took her time. Her hair danced beneath her pink hat. She didn't wear sunglasses or goggles to mar her fresh face. Definitely farm-girl pretty.

"How's she doing?" Ryan had pulled up next to him.

Adam cleared his throat. "Good."

"Thanks, Adam. Thanks for inviting us here."

"No problem." Adam realized he needed this. Spending casual time with Eva might soften the edges a little. Somewhere on the slopes today, she'd stopped looking at him like the enemy.

"I see a guy I work with. I'll be back." Ryan skied toward the lodge.

Adam nodded and waited for Eva.

She picked up speed toward the base of the hill. Weaving around a group of kids who had suddenly stopped in her path, Eva's balance bobbled off kilter. With a squeal, she swooped toward him, coming in too fast.

"Whoa…" He skied toward her, ready to break her fall, when she plowed into him. He wasn't prepared for the force of her impact and slipped. They both went down.

Eva lay sprawled on top of him, laughing. "Sorry."

Adam forced his hands to remain on the ground instead of circling her tiny waist like he wanted. Letting loose a groan, he realized she'd taken him completely out. He'd landed hard on his tailbone.

"I don't weigh that much."

"Wanna bet?" He grinned when her eyes widened.

She was even more appealing close up. That pink hat rode low over her eyebrows, and her nose and cheeks were rosy with sunburn. He couldn't look away. He didn't want to.

"Come on, Peece. You must have girls falling on you all the time."

"Doesn't mean it's all good. There are a lot of gold-digging snits out there. A guy's got to be careful."

Those chocolate-colored eyes of hers widened even more and then she scrambled off him, grazing his shin with her ski.

"Ow. I wasn't calling you one." But the glare in her gaze returned. Just when they'd come to a friendly, comfortable place, Adam had to blow it. Miss Prickly Prim reared her pretty head and looked ready to take a bite.

Just then Ryan approached. "Nice move, Eva, taking out our host. I wanna come back, you know."

"Oh, put a sock in it, Ryan," Eva said as she wobbled to her feet.

He laughed at his sister's retort.

Adam also got up. His shin and his backside had taken a beating, but there was still prime skiing to be had. "How about a couple more runs and then dinner at my place?"

Ryan nodded. "Absolutely."

Eva's brow furrowed. "Skiing's one thing, but we don't expect you to feed us, too. Besides, it's getting late."

"Come on, Eva. I'm hungry."

Adam knew Eva's desire to leave had nothing to do with time and everything to do with his perceived insult. "I have steak that needs to be grilled. You'd be doing me a favor so it won't go to waste."

The pleading look Ryan gave Eva reminded Adam of his own sister and the tug-of-war they'd had over the years. Adam knew how to get his way, as did Ryan. He could see Eva's resolve weaken by the way she chewed her bottom lip.

"Fine. Another run and dinner, but then we've got to go."

* * *

Eva shrugged out of her pink ski suit and handed it to Adam. His fingers touched hers and Eva quickly pulled back. She wouldn't give him any excuse to think she was coming on to him. Not after what he'd said when she fell on him.

Bending down to remove her boots, Eva took her time with the buckles. She didn't want Adam Peece's money. She wanted her orchard back. Wanted to keep it safe and sound. How to do that escaped her.

"Come on, Eva, move it." Ryan was behind her.

She straightened with a huff and kicked off her boots, leaving them in a heap near the coat hooks where Adam had hung their stuff. Walking into the living room, Eva took in the neutral colors and casual fabrics. Furniture covered in denim and leather. Expensive-looking, yet comfortable. Two adjectives she'd never expected to go together.

Padding into Adam's kitchen, she took a deep breath. She'd conquered the mountain today, she could face the man in his den. "Need help?"

"I've got this. Go enjoy the fire." Adam barely looked at her and exited onto the deck through a sliding glass door in the dining room. A huge covered grill area gleamed in stainless steel at the end of the deck. It looked like something from a garden show on TV.

Eva went into the living room and slumped onto the couch while Ryan built a fire in the hearth. She scanned the coffee table. Motorcycles, race cars, farm machinery and ski magazines littered the top.

"Ryan, did you see these?" Eva flipped through an issue about modern farming techniques. She'd have thought Adam would browse men's fashion or sports magazines.

Ryan held up a glossy motorcycle issue. "Gearhead stuff. Pretty funny, huh?"

"You're not kidding." Eva leaned against the pillows and closed her eyes, letting the heat of the fire blanket her. She suddenly felt bone-tired. Her eyelids grew heavy, so she closed her eyes.

She heard Adam come and go through the sliding glass door a couple of times. He asked Ryan how they liked their steaks. The sound of the two of them talking in low tones from the kitchen felt oddly comforting…

"Eva, wake up. Dinner's ready." Ryan jostled her shoulder.

She sat up and rubbed her eyes. "Where's the bathroom?"

"Down the hall," Adam said from the dining room while he set the table.

Eva's stomach rumbled in response to the aroma of Adam's food. From the wonderful smells, she'd guess the guy could cook. And he read greasemonkey magazines. Definitely not what she expected from a pampered green bean heir. "I'll just be a minute."

Adam's hallway looked like a portrait gallery. Family pictures hung everywhere. Eva stopped to inspect a photo that caught her eye. It was Adam as a little boy looking very unhappy about getting his picture taken. He was easy to spot, his brilliant blue eyes gave him away. They were the same shade as a beautiful redhead that stood beside a dark-haired, dark-eyed man who resembled Adam. His parents made a handsome couple.

Then she noticed that several children had their own section of pictures, but Eva zeroed in on Adam's area. His photos captured him engaged in his interests. On a farm tractor as a child, motocross as a teenager, several ski competitions, and even a race-car driving photo mixed in with pictures of Adam atop a big black motorcycle. Adam Peece had done it all.

She quickly found her way to the restroom and returned to sit next to Ryan at the table, putting her across from Adam. "Thank you for dinner. This looks like you know what you're doing."

"It's not rocket science." Adam winked at her.

Once seated, Adam offered up a simple prayer of thanks and Eva was grateful he hadn't asked to hold hands. Her parents still demanded that at mealtime.

One bite of the angel hair pasta in a white wine sauce and Eva was floored by how good it was. And she was ravenous. The three of them ate quickly and quietly. By the time dinner was over, Eva rose to gather plates.

"Don't worry about the dishes, Eva. I can take care of them later."

Her eyebrows rose. "Really Adam, I don't mind. You cooked, I'll clean up."

Eva looked at her brother, whose eyelids were drooping. Maybe she should have left the dishes alone, but it was too late. Ryan was going to crash.

"Do you mind if I sprawl on your couch for a few?" her brother asked.

"Go ahead," Adam said.

Eva placed the dishes by the sink as Adam came in with an armload of bottled salad dressings. She opened the fridge for him, wondering what to say. "When we were kids, Ryan took a nap after dinner to get out of doing the dishes. He's conditioned now. Dinner, then nap."

Adam laughed. "You could have left the dishes for him to do after he woke up."

Eva shrugged. "Even as a kid, I couldn't stand a mess."

They cleared off the table, put away leftovers and loaded the dishwasher in less than fifteen minutes while Ryan snoozed.

"Want some ice cream?"

"Sure." Eva sat on a stool pulled up to the breakfast bar on the other side of the sink. She watched Adam scoop chocolate and coffee ice cream into bowls. He handed one to her, then stayed in the kitchen, leaning against the sink while he dug in.

"Did you have fun with your friends?" Eva gave small talk a try.

Adam shrugged. "It was okay. My college roommates and their wives and some friends got together for a weekend reunion, if you will. One of my school buddy's parents owns a house on West Bay."

"Ah." Eva couldn't think of another question that wouldn't sound as if she was being nosy.

"We're all different guys now. I'm different." Adam took another bite of his ice cream. "Things change."

Eva was all too aware of that. "Yes. They do."

An awkward silence settled between them, until Adam cleared his throat. "Look, Eva, I want to apologize."

"For what?" But she knew.

He set his half-eaten bowl of ice cream on the counter and looked at her. "My comment earlier. I didn't mean to imply anything by it."

Eva set her spoon down with a clink against her bowl. "No big deal."

He didn't look as if he believed her. "I've had my

share of unfortunate encounters, so I've learned to keep my guard up. I'm sorry if I insulted your integrity. That wasn't my intent."

Eva knew all about keeping her guard up, too. Only she'd built a wall, a small fortress really. "It's okay."

Adam ran a hand through his hair. "Good."

She picked up her bowl and took a hearty bite of ice cream. Some of it dribbled down her chin. She searched for a napkin.

"Here." Adam handed her one. His eyes were filled with mirth.

Great, now she looked like a slob.

It hadn't dawned on Eva that people, especially women, would take advantage of him. Her first impression was the other way around. But after spending an afternoon skiing with Adam, and seeing the easy way he had with her and Ryan, those initial thoughts were way off. Adam Peece was a nice guy. A really nice guy. And a believer. For real.

"Are we okay, then?" he asked with a smile.

"Yup." Eva closed her eyes in an attempt to stop the brain freeze blasting through her head from the gigantic spoonful of ice cream she'd practically inhaled.

"Tomorrow. Pruning same time?"

"Eight o'clock." Eva nodded.

Ryan was tied up with meetings, so he wouldn't

be joining them. Eva had no choice but to get used to working alongside Adam. It'd be just the two of them alone in the field. Something she'd better get used to real quick. She had a job to do and she couldn't afford not to do it well.

Chapter Five

Eva checked her watch again. Adam had called and promised to be here by nine. It was past that. He'd taken Friday off to go downstate, and now it was Monday morning—no Adam. The past two weeks, they'd worked well together pruning sweet cherry trees. He'd caught on quickly, eventually bypassing the number of trees she'd trimmed. He enjoyed reminding her of that fact a little too often.

Another peek at the time. Nine twenty. She climbed onto her ATV hooked up to the wagon loaded with gear and started the engine. She wasn't waiting around any longer. He could find his way on his own. Revving the throttle, she pulled out of the garage and then stopped when she spotted Adam's dark blue Jeep pulling in.

He slipped into his coveralls, grabbed his gear and sauntered toward her. He looked pale and there were dark circles under his eyes. "Sorry."

"Rough weekend?" Her voice came out sharper than she'd intended. He'd told her that he'd changed from his old life. Was that a lie?

"What's with you this morning?"

"You look terrible," she said.

His lips curved into a sardonic smile. "Thanks. I don't feel too good, so if we can cut the pleasantries and get started that would be great."

Eva's eyes narrowed. Maybe she should test him and make sure he really had changed. "You're grumpy when you're hungover."

His eyes widened with offense, or maybe it was hurt that she'd think that. "I'm not hungover. I didn't get a good night's sleep because of a killer headache."

"Did you take something? I've got meds in the house." Eva felt a whole lot happier knowing he hadn't been partying. A little guilty, too, for thinking the worst.

"I'm fine. Let's go. The fresh air will help."

"Your four-wheeler is gassed up and ready." Eva smiled.

With a nod, he climbed on and started the engine. Adam Peece was bristly as a bear this morning. He could have skipped today if he felt that bad. He was no different than every male in her family who acted as if they could beat sickness by ignoring it.

Once in the field, Eva kept glancing at Adam working a couple of trees away. The morning had dawned clear with weak winter sunshine filtering through the orchard. The golden haze gave the frosted trees a fairylike glimmer. But Adam, garbed in a down jacket with matching coveralls, made for one overdressed Oberon.

"What?" He caught her watching him.

"Just making sure you're okay."

"I'm fine."

"How was your weekend?" Eva asked.

Adam gave her a wry grin. "My father made himself scarce because his wife and their two kids were sick."

"How old are they?"

"Heather is twenty-nine, Cinda is four and Bella's two."

Eva felt her eyes bulge. She'd meant the kids. "Wait. Heather's your—"

"My dad's wife." Adam sliced a branch as if he had a score to settle with the tree.

"Two little ones in the family must be fun." Eva rebounded from the shock of his stepmother's age with a disconcerting image of Adam bouncing two toddlers on each knee.

"No use backtracking, Eva. I know what you're thinking and, yes, it's weird having a stepmother who's the same age as me."

"Sorry."

"Don't be." A cut branch fell to the ground. "How long have they been married?"

Adam let loose a cynical-sounding laugh. "Four years. Who knows how long this one will last."

Another vicious chop. Then he paused. "That's probably not fair to Heather. She's okay."

Eva moved to the next tree. Climbing her ladder, she had to know. "How many times has your dad been married?"

"Heather is wife number four."

"Four?" Eva breathed.

"He pays alimony to two exes. *Peece Canning Profit Share* takes on new meaning after you've married the boss." Adam's voice dripped scorn.

No wonder Adam wasn't married. "What about your mom?"

His face softened. "She died from cancer when I was nine."

The picture of Adam's mother with all that flaming-red hair and brilliant blue eyes like her son's flashed in her mind with a twinge of sorrow. "I saw a picture of your mom at your town house. I'm really sorry."

"Yeah, me, too. She was a strong woman right up to the end." Even with the distance between them, Eva could read the intensity in his eyes.

"What was her name?"

"Catherine."

Eva couldn't look away from him. "A beautiful name for a beautiful woman. Even though my

parents are miles away, I don't know what I'd do
without either one of them."

"I lost my way for a long while, but I'm back on
the right path. This time I'm staying on it."

"That's good." But her heart ached for him. He'd
been so young when he lost his mother. With his
father's remarriages, it was no wonder Adam kept
his guard up. Another unexpected tidbit of Adam's
life struck a chord within her, making him more
approachable. Even more likeable.

Adam felt as if he'd been talking too much this
morning. With every frosty puff of air, his throat
felt raw, but he didn't want this conversation to end.
"What about you? You grew up in a Christian home.
Did you ever stray from what you'd been taught to
believe in?"

"Not really." Eva looked away from him as she
positioned her loppers around a thin branch.

Her shuttered response made him curious. "No
drunken rebellion? No questioning your purpose in
life?"

"Everyone questions his or her purpose," she
finally said. "Or at least they should."

He cocked his head, pruning completely forgotten. "And what'd you find out?"

She shrugged. "We're designed to have a relationship with God because we're made in His image."

Adam considered her answer a cop-out. Like
Lake Michigan, there were hidden depths to Eva

Marsh. She didn't 'fess up easily, but something about the stiff way she sat during church told him she'd been going through the motions. "Sounds pretty textbook to me. What about the practical stuff?"

"Peece, these sweets won't prune themselves."

He chuckled at her effective shutout. He'd take her *no trespassing* hint even though it made him that much more curious about her. "Now who's grumpy?"

She grinned. "Not me."

"No?" He'd seen the impatient look on her face when he'd pulled in late. This morning's headache found company with aches deep in his muscles about an hour ago. The fresh air wasn't helping. Despite moving around, he couldn't get warm.

Eva let out a sigh. "I'm getting sick of snow. It doesn't help that every time I talk to my folks, my father gives me their weather report. Do you know how warm it is in the Keys right now?"

"Why don't you visit them when we're done pruning? You said yourself there's a bit of a break until the snow melts. We agreed to paid vacation, so why not take it?" He grabbed his milk crate and moved to the next tree.

"Flights out of Traverse City are too expensive."

"So? Fly out of Detroit." He watched Eva make busy work of snapping back straggly branches.

She let out another sigh. "I'm not a fan of the city."

"But you spent a year in New York." He remembered that she'd studied pastry there. He tended to remember a lot about Eva.

"I felt safe in New York."

"What are you afraid of?" The words slipped out before he could catch them. A woman had every reason to be cautious, but catching a flight out of a major airport shouldn't be a big deal.

"I'm the play-it-safe one in the Marsh family and Detroit's a scary place. At least to me." She laughed as if trying to make light of her answer.

"My dad's place has plenty of room if you'd like to stay there instead of a hotel. I'd drive you to the airport. Although, the Peece estate can be a *scary place* with two little girls flying around like a couple of birds and just as noisy."

Her eyes widened. "Look, Peece—"

He felt as surprised as she looked. He'd never invited a woman to his father's home before, but he wanted his family to meet Eva. Maybe it was about proving to his dad that he could work with an attractive woman and not get involved. Or to show his sister that he knew a nice girl. Not that he was looking. His faith felt too fragile to risk losing it with an ill-timed relationship.

Besides, Eva was the last person he should consider getting involved with. Not when the orchard was already between them. What if he failed to break even this season? He had a pretty good idea that she'd never forgive him if he lost this land. The deal with his father was something Eva need never know. He'd prove himself, and Marsh Orchards would be all his. Until then, he'd be wise to keep his relationship with Eva friendly but professional.

Still, he gave her a wink. "Think about it."

By midafternoon, visiting her parents was all Eva could think about. There was no way she'd take Adam up on his gracious offer. Staying with his family would be way too weird. She'd feel out of place. Really, how would Adam introduce her? As his farm manager or his employee?

She glanced at Adam with concern. He hadn't eaten much at lunch and he'd gotten awfully quiet. "Hey, are you okay?"

"I don't know." Adam sat on his milk crate and hung his head in his hands.

She pushed through the shin-deep snow until she stood in front of him. "What's wrong?"

He lolled his head back so he could look up at her. The normally golden-olive tone of his skin held a sickly gray hue that wasn't there this morning. "I feel lightheaded."

"Because you didn't eat." Without hesitation, Eva slipped off her glove and touched his forehead with the back of her hand. "You're hot."

With a weak attempt at a grin Adam said, "I'm glad you think so."

Eva rolled her eyes, but her stomach did a flip of its own. Even sick, the guy could charm. "Come on, Peece. Let's call it quits for today. I think you're running a fever."

Adam groaned when he bent to pick up his crate.

"Can you drive the four-wheeler?"

"'Course I can." He looked offended by her questioning his ability.

But Adam drove through the orchard at a snail's pace. A sure sign that he was truly ill. Why hadn't he stayed home today? What a classic stubborn guy thing to do—coming to work when he didn't feel good.

After they pulled into the garage, Adam was slow to climb off the ATV. She sidled next to him. "Here, lean on me."

"I can walk." He pushed at her shoulder with the strength of a two-year-old.

"Maybe so, but if you pass out, there's no way I can get you inside without help and Beth won't be home for another hour." She shifted his arm around her shoulders, breathing in the smell of winter air and ATV exhaust that still clung to both of them.

Adam didn't look pleased about the situation. He looked uncomfortable and maybe even a little embarrassed. "I thought I could beat it."

Eva couldn't help but chuckle. "You know what they say, 'Pride cometh before a fall.'"

"Yeah, yeah, yeah."

They made their way up the steps and into the house. Eva slipped off her outer garments while Adam wandered into the living room.

He slumped onto the couch. "I just need to lie here for a few minutes."

Eva tossed kindling and small logs into the fireplace, then lit the pile with a match. The snap and crackle of flames licking the wood was the only sound in the quiet farmhouse. She glanced at Adam. His eyes were closed.

Bending over him, she gently slipped off his gloves and hat. When he didn't stir, Eva unlaced his boots and dropped them to the floor. Even his wool socks looked expensive. She tucked his feet onto the couch and covered him with a thick throw blanket.

She touched his forehead again, fighting the urge to smooth back his hair and kiss his brow. What now?

"Thanks, Eva," Adam croaked.

"You should take off your coat."

"Just a quick nap and then I'll head home."

Eva knew better. Adam was in no condition to drive an hour to his town house. Whatever illness his little half sisters had suffered, he'd caught the same flu bug. And that meant he wouldn't be fine any time soon.

"How is he?" Beth sat at the kitchen table with her schoolwork spread out around her.

"He's still sleeping on the couch." Eva glanced at the clock. It'd been almost three hours. Worry nagged her. She'd given him water and a pain reliever to fight the fever, but he'd zonked back out. "Should I wake him up?"

Beth shrugged.

"Eva?"

She turned toward the sound of Adam's craggy voice, and her stomach pitched with dread.

He leaned against the kitchen's entryway. His face looked mottled and blotchy, his eyes glassy, his lips swollen. "What did you give me?"

Her mind went blank and then she remembered. "Ibuprofen."

His eyes closed. "I'm allergic to it."

"Why didn't you say something?" Her voice sounded shrill as she flew out of her chair and rushed toward him. Oh, what had she done?

"We've got to get him to the emergency room," Beth said.

"No, no. Got any Benedryl?" He was in his stocking feet, but still wore his coat and coveralls. He'd been too chilled to remove them. His sweat-soaked hair plastered his head.

Eva looked at Beth, but her roommate slipped on her coat and grabbed her purse. "Where are you going?"

"I'll get the car. Eva, get Adam ready and let's go." Beth knew how to spot allergic reactions as part of her training as an elementary teacher. If she thought this was serious, it was.

Eva swallowed hard as she stared at Adam. "I'll get your boots."

Five minutes later, Eva slammed the back door of Beth's car and climbed into the passenger seat. She turned to keep her eye on Adam, who sprawled in the backseat. He wasn't saying much, and he kept swallowing as if he were having trouble breathing. The nearest emergency room was twenty miles away in Traverse City. What if—

"Dear Lord, please let him be okay," she whispered.

"Amen." Beth sped up.

They made it to the hospital in record time, despite the wintry road conditions. Eva rushed inside the E.R. with Adam while Beth parked.

"Oh, man, this isn't good." Adam tossed his wallet at Eva and then clutched his stomach.

With shaking hands, she gave the E.R. nurse his insurance card and driver's license. "He's having an allergic reaction to ibuprofen."

They got him in to see a doctor right away, while Eva stayed behind filling out Adam's paperwork to the best of her ability. Slipping into a vinyl chair that crinkled when she sat down, Eva tapped her pen against her leg. She had no clue about Adam's health history.

"How is he?" Beth flopped into the seat next to her.

"I don't know." Concentrating on the form attached to a clipboard, Eva let out a groan. "Immediate family? Beth, I don't even know who to call in an emergency."

"Check his coat and see if his cell is in there."

Eva found Adam's phone tucked into an inside pocket. Holding the state-of-the-art phone in her hand, she hesitated. "Maybe I should wait. We don't know anything yet, and what if he doesn't want me calling his family?"

Beth shook her head. "Check his contact list. If you need to make a call, it's best to be prepared. You can jot the numbers on that form."

Sucking her lip between her teeth, Eva flipped the phone and scanned the menu until she found Adam's contact list. Scrolling through dozens of names, she couldn't ignore how many of them were women's names. A twinge of unease that felt too much like jealousy flitted through her.

And finally, a number tagged "Dad." She jotted it down.

"What if he freaks out about me giving him those pills and fires me?"

"He's not going to fire you, Eva. It was an honest mistake. You were just trying to help."

A LeNaro News headline flashed through her mind. *Local grower killed by employee's good intentions.* Nice.

Beth threw her arm around her and gave her a squeeze. "Quit worrying. He's going to be fine, Eva."

Maybe Eva exaggerated, but she was responsible for bringing him here. Why hadn't she asked Adam before she slipped those two little tablets in his mouth? He'd been so out of it, he hadn't said a word. Who was allergic to ibuprofen, anyway?

"Are you Mrs. Peece?" A nurse asked.

Eva felt like a deer blinded by bright headlights. "No. No. I mean, we brought him in."

"The doctor would like to talk with you."

Eva's gut clenched when she stood.

"I'm coming, too." Beth grabbed Eva's cold hand.

Eva squared her shoulders. She'd face the consequences as hers alone, but it still felt good having Beth's support.

Walking into one of the E.R. examining rooms, Eva heard Adam's groan before spotting him lying flat on the bed with his arm over his eyes. She glanced at the doctor. "Is he okay?"

The doctor introduced himself and shook her hand. "He's going to be out of it, but he'll be fine. He threw up most of those meds, but the shot of epinephrine I gave him should speed whatever's left out of his system. Here's another dose in case, but I think he'll sleep it off."

Eva's knees went rubbery with relief. "Rest."

"And water or juice and maybe some food in the morning if he feels up to it. He's all yours, ladies."

Eva nodded. She owed him a gourmet breakfast for this one. Stepping close, she touched Adam's elbow. "Peece?"

Nothing.

"Adam?" It came out a breathy whisper.

His eyes opened, but he looked groggy. "What?"

She smiled. He wore the same surly expression as the little boy he'd been in the picture hanging on the wall in his townhome. "Ready?"

"Yeah."

Eva looked at Beth. "We better have Ryan meet us at home to get him upstairs."

Before Eva could hope to fall asleep, she needed to make sure Adam was okay. Ryan had to practically carry the guy upstairs. Considering the fever and throwing up in the E.R., Eva made sure Ryan brought down Adam's clothes so she could wash them. The first exercise in trying to make up for what she'd done.

She slipped into her parents' old room and padded quietly to the trunk at the foot of the bed. Setting down Adam's neatly folded and cleaned clothes, she looked at him lying perfectly still in the middle of the queen-size bed.

A nightlight from the connecting bathroom threw shadows on the far wall. She remembered as a kid climbing in between her mom and dad whenever she'd been scared or had a bad dream. After Todd, Eva had been tempted to do the same thing more than a few times.

Funny that she felt safe around Adam. Protected. She stepped closer to him, her heart filled with concern. Was he breathing?

She narrowed her eyes, trying to see if his chest rose and fell, but the covers were drawn up over his shoulders. The bedspread looked smooth, as if he hadn't moved an inch since climbing into bed. His dark hair draped the pillow, framing his head, but he didn't look peaceful in sleep.

Eva stepped closer and placed her hand near his nose. Air went in and then came out. A stray swirl of his hair distracted her from pulling back. Begging to be smoothed, Eva reached for it.

He grabbed her wrist.

She squealed. "You scared me!"

"*Me* scare you? What are you doing in here?" He

let go and sat up. The deep tone of his skin looked even darker against the blinding-white sheets. A silver chain hung around his neck with a tiny medical alert charm dangling against the center of his chest. A little late for *that* now.

She clutched the side of her neck, feeling the heat crawl up her skin. She tried to catch her breath and tried even harder to look away from the man in front of her. But failed on all counts.

"I wanted—" She wanted to touch his hair? "I wanted to make sure you were still breathing. Don't you move around when you sleep?"

"How should I know? I'm asleep." He still looked a little dazed but also amused if the quirk of his lips was any indication.

"Right." Eva laughed, and it sounded loud and awkward. But then she was standing in a bedroom with her *boss*. Picking up an empty glass from the nightstand, she headed for the bathroom. "I'll refill this for you."

"Eva, I'm fine."

She returned with the water. Setting the glass gingerly on the table, she chanced a peek at Adam. "I'm so sorry about this."

He held up his hand. "We can talk about it in the morning."

"Okay." She hurried to the armoire and pulled out a handmade quilt to drape across the foot of the bed. "In case you get cold. My cousin Steve made this with Grandma Marsh. Pretty cool, huh?"

He smiled. "Good night, Eva."

She felt her face flush. "Good night, Peece."

Adam woke in the morning feeling oddly refreshed if a little weak. He'd slept ten hours straight according to his watch. Wait, that ten hours had been interrupted by a midnight check from Eva that had spooked him. Like an apparition from a ghost story, he'd woken to her hand hovering near his mouth. The memory of her huge eyes had him wondering if she'd been real or a product of his dreams.

He flung the covers back and stepped onto the chilly hardwood floor. Weak light filtered into the room. Shuffling to the window, he peeked through lace curtains. Big fat snowflakes fell, blanketing the orchard in yet another layer of white.

Adam needed to get out there and help finish the pruning. Eva had probably started without him. He ran his hand through his hair and knew a shower was his first priority.

When he stepped downstairs, instead of finding the kitchen empty, Eva leaned against the counter wearing a baggy sweatshirt over even baggier flannel pajama bottoms spotted with pink poodles. She sipped coffee and stared at a warm fire bobbing in the woodstove. The place smelled like vanilla and cinnamon.

"Hey."

Eva's eyes widened and she immediately straightened. "How do you feel?"

"Much better. And thanks for washing my clothes."

"It's the least I could do after—"

"Poisoning me?" He liked they way her cheeks turned rosy-red.

"Why didn't you tell me you were allergic?"

He shrugged. "I don't know. They looked like Tylenol to me, so I just figured they were."

She gave him a sad expression as if she'd run over someone's cat. "I feel terrible. What if you went into shock or something?"

"I did, but you girls saved the day."

"Beth's good at that. She's quick in a crisis. Maybe it's a teacher thing. Speaking of which, we need to exchange our emergency contact info in case something happens to either of us in the field."

Adam narrowed his eyes. "You're serious."

"Of course, I am. Accidents happen, you know. My grandfather accidentally shot himself while cleaning his gun. I was only five when he died, but it still makes me think. You can't be too careful."

"I guess not." So far with Eva he'd been the only one who ended up in pain. But she made a good point. He hoped they never had to execute an emergency call. He should have thought of it when they started working together. "Got a pen and paper?"

"Yup. I printed out mine for you." She pushed a couple pieces of paper toward him and then looked up. "Are you hungry?"

"Yes," he said quietly. Eva's hair hadn't been combed and it hung in a tousled mess past her shoulders. Her cheek still bore a crease from her pillow. His fingers itched to smooth that tiny red line on her face. He slammed his hands into his pockets.

Finding her cute was one thing, but this attraction to her was definitely something else. He should hightail it out fast, but his feet felt nailed to the floor. "Are we pruning later then?"

She shook her head. "Not today. I think you should go home and rest. I've got some personal stuff I need to take care of anyway."

He nodded but couldn't help but wonder what she was up to today.

"Coffee?" She turned to get a mug from the cupboard and then handed it to him.

His fingers slid over hers. "Thanks."

She gave him a searching look before pulling away, and then she got busy pouring the strong brew in his cup. "The E.R. doctor gave me an extra dose of epinephrine. Make sure I give it to you before you leave."

"Keep it here." He grinned. "Just in case you slip me another mickey."

Her eyes widened, and her full-lipped mouth dropped open.

"I'm teasing you, Eva."

She shook her head. "Not funny. I could have killed you."

"But you didn't."

With a slight smile she said, "I have a new recipe for you to try if you're up for it. Baked cherry pecan French toast stuffed with sweet ricotta cheese. It'll be done in a couple minutes."

"Sounds amazing." Eva and cherries. He couldn't think of one without the other. "Did you remodel the room I stayed in?"

"That was my parents' room. And yes, I wallpapered and painted and found some comfy furniture at a yard sale. I planned on making it the main suite. The other three bedrooms need private baths installed."

"That'll be expensive." He sat on a stool on the other side of the island, content to sip his coffee and watch her put out plates and silverware.

She shrugged. "I'll figure out a way."

The clunk-clunk of Beth coming down the stairs prevented Adam from prying into how Eva planned to do that. Her plans were none of his business.

"Morning, Adam. How are you feeling?" Beth

grabbed a cup of coffee and slipped into a chair next to his.

"Better."

"Did Eva tell you the news?" Beth stirred two heaping teaspoons of sugar into her coffee.

"What news is that?" He watched Eva stuff her hands into oven mitts and pull a steaming pan out of the oven.

"I'm going with her to see her folks. We're flying out of Cherry Capital Airport in Traverse City."

He wasn't surprised, but the quick stab of disappointment he experienced was far from expected. "When?"

"Less than two weeks is spring break. We got a great deal. My mother works at the airport."

"That's great." Adam figured that Eva wasn't the kind of person who'd pull in a favor from Beth's mother on her own. She certainly hadn't taken him up on his offer, but he hadn't expected her to. He couldn't believe he'd thrown it out there.

The fact that Eva wouldn't look at him while she sliced into her French toast confirmed a stubborn desire to do things on her own, without help. He appreciated her independence. He practiced it, too.

Eva served both Adam and Beth and then waited for their reactions. She'd baked this for Adam, really. Exercise number two in trying to make up for putting him in the emergency room. The golden hue of his skin had returned. His shower-damp hair and stubble-lined jaw made him look strong and healthy. A far cry from the man who'd crashed on her couch yesterday. "Well?"

"This is excellent, Eva." Beth was the first to give her opinion.

"Amazing," Adam said. "You'll make the perfect B and B hostess."

"Thank you." Eva's insides swirled at the compliment. And then she glanced at Beth, who grinned at her.

Great. Was it obvious? That something had changed. That she liked taking care of Adam. Making him breakfast, washing his clothes…

"Well, I'd better go or be late for school." Beth gulped her coffee.

Eva held her breath as she watched Beth leave. The silence her roommate left behind throbbed in Eva's ears. Or maybe it was that sharp awareness that she and Adam were all alone. What now? She exhaled with a short sigh.

"I'd better go, too." Adam finished the last of his French toast.

Eva walked him to the door as if an invisible string had been tied from him to her. "You sure you're okay?"

Of course he was okay, better than okay. He looked great. And she couldn't think of a single intelligent thing to say. A new apprehension filled the space of the kitchen, making the air hum and her pulse beat harder. Could he hear the thumping going on inside her chest?

"I'm fine."

She wrinkled her nose. "I'm glad you didn't fire me."

"For what?" He gently tugged on a strand of her hair. "I can't fire you, Eva. I need you."

The warmth in his voice made her breath catch. But he was talking about the orchard. He needed her experience. That was all.

But could he need more?

Chapter Six

❧

"This is awesome." Eva ignored the tightening sensation of the skin on her shoulders from the hot Florida sunshine. Lying on a floatie in her parents' pool, she paddled close to her dad, also in a floating lounger with a thriller paperback in his hands.

He wore a floppy hat and white zinc oxide on his nose, but she couldn't tell if he *really* enjoyed living here. Her folks had rented a nice little home with a pool as a test of their aptitude for retirement. Eva wasn't sure they were old enough to retire. A fine-looking, healthy couple in their mid and late fifties, her parents seemed a little out of place in the land of cotton tops. But the Keys were different. Not so elderly, Eva mused.

"We're glad you're here, cupcake. And Beth, too." Her father smiled.

Eva glanced at her friend snoozing on a lounge

chair with her paperback novel draped across her middle.

"Bob?" Eva's mom stepped out onto the patio. "Phone call."

"Who is it?"

Her mother gave him a pointed look, and Eva couldn't begin to guess what that was all about. And then her mother finally said, "It's Adam."

Eva's mouth dropped open and she rose up on her elbows, tipping her rubber mat in the process.

Her father slipped out of the pool and into the house.

"What's he want?" Eva asked her mom.

"I don't know, honey."

A slice of worry cut through her. She hoped nothing was wrong. Slipping into the water, Eva swam to the ladder and got out. Grabbing a towel, she went inside to find out why Adam had called.

Her dad was just finishing the call by the time she found him outside on the front stoop.

"What's up?"

"Adam had a question about dewinterizing the well head."

"Why didn't he ask for me?" Eva stared at two white birds walking around the corner of the house across the street.

"Could you answer his question about getting the water systems ready to go?"

Eva scrunched her nose. "Not really."

"Well, there you go. Plus he didn't want to bother you on vacation."

"Oh, so it's okay to bother you?"

Her dad laughed. "Yes. Now, tell me how he's doing."

Eva sighed. Adam was doing better than she'd expected. He'd been focused on pruning, but would his interest fade when the work got tougher? "He seemed to enjoy dormant pruning."

"But?" Her father seemed to sense her reservations.

She shrugged and nearly winced. She'd been in the sun too long. "But what's to keep him from bailing? I mean, what's a guy like him doing with our orchard?"

Her father chuckled as he gazed out over the tropical-looking neighborhood. "Do you think I would have sold the farm to someone I didn't think belonged there? To someone who wouldn't love it like we do?"

Eva glanced at her dad. Of course he still loved the farm, but Adam Peece? He wasn't one of them. He wasn't even a local who understood the risks of fruit farming. "What makes you think he's got what it takes?"

Her father shrugged. "Just a hunch when I watched him drink in his first view of the land. It had been after the harvest, Eva, when the trees aren't pretty like blossom time. The man's eyes glowed."

Eva shook her head. With Adam's bright blue eyes, maybe her father had mistaken the play of light as something more. Or maybe it was greed. Adam wouldn't have bought the orchard if he didn't want it. But after a full season, would he still?

By the first full week in April, Adam understood why Eva called it the *mud season*. Slogging through the early April mess of melting snow, Adam experienced what she meant. Mud spattered his Jeep and covered his work boots, and the brown stuff congealed near the entrance of the pole barn. He found his farm manager inside peering into a big ole John Deere tractor engine.

Only a week had passed since he'd last worked with Eva, but she hadn't been far from his thoughts after she'd gone to Florida. Seeing her jump-started his pulse. Not a good thing when Adam knew keeping it professional was the sensible route.

Adam couldn't run this farm by himself, not yet anyway. Getting romantically involved with Eva would make working together difficult. Eva had already demonstrated that she didn't take breakups lightly, so why go there? He wasn't about to risk losing not only his teacher but also the needed guidance from her father. Nope, there was too much riding on his breaking even at the end of the season.

He noticed that Eva had dressed for working outdoors—jeans and a sweatshirt. Even her mud-speckled rubber boots had cherries on them. His sister would label them farm-chic. To him, Eva was farm-girl cute.

"Problems?" he finally said.

She dropped a wrench on the cement floor and then looked up with a grin. "Must you sneak up on a person?"

"You knew I'd be here at nine." Adam picked up the tool and handed it over without taking his eyes off her face. She'd been in the sun and the results were mesmerizing. Tanned farm girl registered way higher than cute.

Eva shrugged. "I wasn't watching the clock and I certainly didn't hear you."

"Small wonder." He reached for a radio sitting on the workbench and turned down the blaring pop song.

She made a face and wiped her hands on the back of worn jeans that hugged her figure. "After all this time off, is nine o'clock too early for you?"

He laughed. "I didn't take time off."

Her eyebrows rose. "You didn't?"

"Nope. I organized the barn by setting up an office space, dewinterized the water systems—"

"You really should call me and not my dad, you know. I'm the one you're paying."

He'd paid her father a pretty penny, too. Or rather his father, Leonard Peece, had. If Adam succeeded this season, his father would sign off on Adam cashing in his shares to pay off that note. If he failed, his dad took the orchard. And Leonard Peece had no intention of farming it.

"I'll keep that in mind." But he had no intention of cutting communications with Bob Marsh. Adam needed all the help he could get. "I also pruned those young sweets with Ryan's help."

"They're done?"

"Done." He expected her to be pleased, but Adam got the distinct feeling that she wasn't, as if he'd done something special without her. Left her out on purpose and overstepped a boundary, which was ridiculous.

"Good. So, what kind of music do you like?"

He didn't get the sudden change of subject. "You're okay that I pruned the trees?"

Eva shrugged, but she glanced at the floor. "Yeah, sure. Absolutely."

Did he misread her? He didn't think so.

She looked back up at him with a challenge in her eyes. "Big-city boy like you, I'd say jazz."

He'd play her game. "Not even close."

Eva chewed her plump bottom lip for a second.

"Hmm. You don't look like the country type, definitely not heavy metal…"

He turned the radio dial until he found what he was looking for and upped the volume. Spreading his hands wide, he sighed with pleasure. "Classic rock."

Eva pretended to yawn. "Bo-ring."

"You're crazy. Those bands had distinction instead of the sound-just-like-everyone-else fluff you were listening to."

"You can't dance to rock."

"Sure you can." He'd never have guessed that Miss Prickly Prim liked to dance. Eva swaying with the music would be worth seeing. This time he changed the subject. "So, how was your trip?"

"Relaxing. My parents send their hellos, and my dad asked how I thought you were doing."

"How'd you answer?"

"I said it was still wait-and-see but I gave you a B-plus for pruning."

Adam laughed. "You're pretty tough on grading, especially since I earned extra credit by pruning the young trees."

She gave him a saucy smirk. "I don't dole out As on easy activities."

Hard-nosed. She didn't like it that he pruned faster than her. "So, what's the deal with the tractor?"

Eva shrugged. "It won't start."

"Let me see." It was his tractor. He might as well

get to know it. He'd purchased most of the heavy equipment that went with the orchard, but the three ATVs belonged to Eva.

Adam climbed into the cockpit and turned the key. Nothing. The engine turned over, but no spark of ignition. Plugs? He stepped down and peered under the hood.

"Do you know what you're doing?"

He flashed her a grin. "A motor's a motor."

"And you know a motor from where? Your magazines?"

Was there ever a sharper tongue? But the twinkle in Eva's eyes gave her away. She was baiting him. Throwing down another challenge he wasn't about to back away from. "I tinker."

"If your tinkering doesn't work, I'll call someone."

"Oh ye of little faith," Adam called out to her departing back.

Twenty minutes later when the tractor roared to life, he spotted Eva in the doorway with a basket over her arm. "You did it."

He shut it off and wiped his hands on a rag. Feeling pretty proud of himself, he bowed. "There you go, ma'am."

She gave him an odd look. "Great, let's hook up the wagon and get to work."

Back to business. No fawning, no pat on the back.

He craved a little praise here. "What're we doing today, field boss?"

"Picking up the branches from pruning. Once that's done, we usually have a big bonfire with some neighboring growers. Kind of like a kickoff to the growing season. Are you interested?"

He loved the idea. "Absolutely. What's in the basket?"

"Coffee and muffins."

"With dried cherries?"

She looked away. "And chocolate chips."

Something about the way her cheeks flushed confirmed that she'd baked those muffins for him. Eva was a person of action. Her gratitude popped out of the oven instead of her mouth. "After clearing the brush, what's next?"

"Applying nitrogen fertilizers throughout the whole orchard, and then dormant spraying for bacterial canker. There's also a section of old trees you need to decide what you're going to do with."

She might be more comfortable talking work than anything else, but there was something softer about Eva. Maybe it was her vacation or the mild spring weather. Whatever the cause, he liked it. And he liked her. A lot.

After hours spent gathering brush and branches, Eva was worn-out. Dropping a large bundle onto the trailer, she stretched her back.

"Ready to call it a day?" Adam leaned against the tractor tire looking like a city boy on a country field trip. His leather jacket was dirty and the cuffs of his jeans were mud-splattered. He wore a Detroit Tigers hat and his dark hair curled up at the ends.

She wanted to touch that hair and feel its texture. Eva released a weary sigh. "We'll finish the brush tomorrow and then start fertilizing the orchard. How's Friday night for the bonfire?"

"Friday's perfect. Hey, you said something about old trees. Where are they?"

Eva shook off her wayward thoughts. "I'll show you."

Adam held the tractor cockpit door open for her. "You drive. I'll hang on."

She climbed in and lowered the window to give Peece something more substantial to grasp while he balanced on the tractor step. Did he find the closeness in the cockpit uncomfortable, too?

In no time they were at the back of the orchard where trees planted before she'd been born grew. Her father had never gotten around to removing them. She shut off the motor. "This is it. Might as well be seven acres of firewood."

Adam jumped down from the tractor step and looked around. "These are big trees."

"Worthless."

He gave her a swift look. "So, they're old."

"They no longer produce much fruit. They served

their purpose, but it's time to uproot them, refurbish the soil and let it sit a couple years before replanting."

"More Montmorency?"

At least he knew the name of the tart cherries they grew. "Whatever you prefer."

His eyes narrowed. "And what would you do?"

Without a moment's hesitation, Eva jumped in with her opinion. "Sweets—I'd plant more sweet cherries. I think that's where the money's at for a small orchard."

"How so?"

"There are more retail outlets for selling sweet cherries. Fruit stands, farmers' markets in Traverse City, U-pick." Eva had tried to convince her father of this very thing, but he was used to doing business his way. The same way for years and look where it had gotten him. Forced to retire because he couldn't compete with the big commercial orchards.

Adam took off his hat and fingercombed his hair. "I don't have to decide this year."

Eva disagreed. "Leaving unproductive crop in the field wastes time and money."

He smiled. "These trees are the least of my worries. Come on, let's head back and unload this brush where you want it."

Eva followed Adam to the tractor, wondering why he didn't recognize the urgency of setting up a plan now so they'd be ready to plant when the time came.

If only the orchard were still hers. Then she'd have a stronger voice on how things were done. As an employee, she was no better off than she'd been as a daughter trying to convince her father of her ideas.

An idea blossomed in her brain of sheer genius. With the right approach, would Adam consider taking her on as a partner? She couldn't afford much of a buy-in, but even a small percentage of ownership might go a long way toward protecting the orchard. She had her B and B to consider. Other than her unique baking with cherries, comfortable lodging on a working cherry farm was her plan to draw guests.

She smiled. A partnership offer was definitely worth a shot.

"When's Adam coming to the bonfire?" Beth asked.

Eva shrugged. "He's bringing someone he wants me to meet."

Aunt Jamee set down a tray of bite-size sandwiches on a checkered cloth-covered table that had been set up in the orchard's pole barn. "Who's he bringing? A girl?"

"I don't know. Maybe it's his father. They're up this weekend." But a worm of concern wiggled around her insides. He wouldn't bring a date, would he?

The Marsh bonfire had become something of an institution. Several growers, even the nearby vineyard owners, came together on Marsh land to celebrate the arrival of spring.

"Don't worry, Jamee," Beth added. "I think our Mr. Peece is interested in Eva."

Eva rolled her eyes, but her belly did a little somersault. "He's not into me."

Her aunt grinned as if she'd stumbled upon a juicy secret. "Why shouldn't he be? Take a look in the mirror, my beauty."

Eva smiled at her aunt's endearment, but Adam was bringing someone. Surely he would have told her if he was dating someone. Wouldn't he?

Eva looked up in time to see Adam walking toward her with a gorgeous dark-haired woman wearing ridiculously high-heeled boots. And her heart sank.

Her aunt's expression simply said that's-a-shame, while Beth's hard stare might as well have shot daggers at Adam.

"Hey," Adam said when he stood before her.

The raven-haired beauty also had dark eyes that focused so intensely on her, Eva backed up a step.

"Eva, I want to you to meet my sister, Anne." Adam smiled.

His sister!

Of course it was his sister. The resemblance suddenly shone clearly. The intensity of her gaze was so similar to Adam's. And Eva remembered seeing a picture of this woman at the town house. Eva's shoulders dipped with relief. "It's really nice to meet you."

Anne grasped her extended hand with surprising strength. "It's nice to finally meet you. We wondered who'd be brave enough to take Adam on as a pupil."

Eva glanced at Beth, whose smile couldn't have been broader. "Why's that?"

Anne grinned, making her look even more like Adam. "He's got a short attention span. He gets bored easily and doesn't stick with stuff."

Eva looked at Adam to see how he'd take his sister's ribbing.

He gave Anne an indulgent smile, but Eva could tell the last statement rubbed him wrong when the corner of his eye twitched. "Just because I can't sit still in meetings doesn't mean I don't listen and learn. It means I don't belong there."

Eva could clearly envision Adam fidgeting in a boardroom. But when Anne looked ready to disagree, Eva stepped in. "Let me show you around and introduce you both. This is my roommate, Beth, and my aunt Jamee. Oh, and this is my uncle Larry. He's our beekeeper."

Anne extended her slender hand to everyone.

When she reached Uncle Larry, her eyebrows shot up. "Beekeeper?"

Uncle Larry smiled, proud to explain his duties. "Sweet cherries don't self-pollinate. Come blossom time, we bring over the bees."

Eva glanced at Adam and read the gratitude in his eyes. But she couldn't shake what Anne had said about her brother. Adam didn't follow through. Not a good thing. Not at all.

She turned her attention back to the conversation.

"We place the beehives in the orchard for a week or so. They get fruit, and we get honey along with a rental fee on the bees," her uncle explained.

"You'll have to bake me something so I can try this cherry blossom honey," Adam said softly to Eva.

His request had been phrased as if they'd been alone. Eva felt her cheeks heat as the stares of everyone bored into her. It was out in the open now. She baked for Adam. "Absolutely. Sure."

She glanced at Aunt Jamee, who raised one perfectly arched eyebrow. But Eva hurried Adam and his sister toward the other guests before her aunt had the chance to state the obvious. Something more than muffins simmered between Eve and Adam.

As the fire blazed with sparks towering into the cool night air, Eva watched Adam work the party like a pro. He chatted with Jim Sandborn and another grower from a few miles north. The men laughed, and Eva could tell they were beginning to accept Adam. Trust might be a ways off yet, but then, she didn't fully trust Adam either.

Sipping hot chocolate, Eva smiled when Ryan's marshmallow caught on fire. The smell of burning sugar wafted toward her in the soft breeze and she breathed deep. She loved the annual bonfire and hoped this wasn't the last one. As long as Adam stuck it out, there could be more. There had to be more.

Anne tiptoed toward her, careful to keep her heels from sinking into the moist grass. With a laugh, she said, "I wore the wrong shoes."

Anne was decked out in designer jeans and a long gray coat over a simple knit turtleneck. Just like Adam, she looked as if she'd stepped off the pages of a glossy magazine.

"The ground's still wet from the snowmelt." Eva stood in the entrance of the pole barn.

The pile of branches had a while to burn down, yet Ryan threw on more logs. The warmth of the fire and the mild spring evening fostered folks' desire to linger. Beth pointed out star constellations to a couple of kids who sat enraptured with her knowledge.

"Now I understand why Adam loves this property. It's beautiful. I'd build a house right over there.

With the view of the lakes, it'd be perfect for a summer place." Anne pointed toward the crest of a hill where the orchard began.

Eva squeezed her empty cup until her thumb poked a hole through the Styrofoam. "Yeah."

"Your home is lovely, too."

Eva got the feeling Anne had left off the phrase *for an old house*. Adam's sister struck her as a gotta-have-new kind of girl. "Thanks."

"It reminds me of our grandparents' place. Adam used to spend hours in the field with Grandpa during our summer visits. They had a small farm not too far from the condo. But Adam must have told you all that."

"Not really." That explained a lot when it came to Adam's approach to the orchard. His kid-on-vacation eagerness suddenly made sense.

Anne smiled. "Growing up, all Adam ever wanted to be was a farmer like Grandpa. Drove my dad nuts. Then, in high school, he wanted to be a mechanic. Again, not something suited for a Peecetorini, if you know what I mean."

Eva didn't. "Peece-tor-eeni?"

"Our real name. The family name. Dad had it legally shortened to match the business after mom died."

"Oh." Eva silently rolled the name around on her tongue. She caught Adam's gaze from the other side of the fire. His family name suited him. Peecetorini was a beautiful name for a beautiful man.

"I've got a great idea," Anne said. "Why don't you and your brother come for dinner tomorrow night? The girls would love it. They're show-offs for company."

Eva bit her lip. "Yeah, sure, as long as we won't be an imposition."

Anne waved her hand. "We eat around seven, so come down just before then. Oh, and bring your friend Beth, too."

"Okay, we will." Eva wanted to know more about the stuff Adam had a history of not sticking with. Was it just hobbies or life in general?

Adam spotted Anne talking to Eva and he wondered what tales his sister might be telling. She'd badgered him all day about Eva. What was she like? And what was Adam planning to do with her? Ignoring his sister was usually the wisest course. For a woman who vowed to stay single, Anne's mind had a determinedly romantic slant. She'd thrown dozens of her friends his way, but Adam hadn't gone out with a single one. He didn't want to put Anne in the middle of his love life.

If Adam explained the reasons why a romance with his farm manager would never work, Anne might push harder. A nice Christian woman was exactly what Adam needed, according to Anne.

And that was probably true, but now wasn't the time.

He made his way toward the two. "Well, it's getting late. Eva, can we help you with anything before we go?"

"Go?" Anne looked at him as if he'd sprouted a second head. "Adam, it's only nine thirty."

Eva waved her hand in dismissal. "Go ahead. There's very little to clean up."

"Thanks, Eva, for giving me the opportunity to meet some of the area growers in a relaxed environment. I appreciate it." The mistrust wasn't gone but definitely eased.

"You're welcome."

"Jim Sandborn invited me to attend the IPM meetings coming up."

"You'll learn a lot." Eva's eyes looked wary, and he couldn't begin to guess why.

"What's IPM?" Anne asked.

"Integrated Pest Management," Adam and Eva said together.

"Eww, bugs! Do you have to kill bugs?" His sister wrinkled her nose.

He glanced at Eva, who smiled. "More than bugs. These meetings are about protecting the orchard from leaf spot, diseases, excessive spraying. That kind of thing."

"Don't forget repelling wildlife. Namely, birds and deer," Eva added.

His sister shook her head. "You sure you want to do this, Adam? It's a wonder we get any cherries at all."

Adam glanced at Eva and her brow furrowed. She didn't think he'd last. What did he expect when his own family thought he'd gone crazy? "Therein lies the challenge."

"I hope you're up for it," Anne said.

Adam watched Eva control her expression. He'd prove to her he could be a good grower. He'd prove it to all of them as long as he broke even. "It's in my blood, Anne. Great-gramps mastered green beans, I'll master cherries. With Eva's help."

Anne looped her arm around Eva for a quick squeeze. "Good luck, Eva. You're going to need it."

To his surprise, Eva didn't shrug away from his sister. She draped her arm around Anne's waist and then gave him a shrewd stare. "Not to worry, I have a plan."

Adam would be a liar if he didn't admit to the drop of alarm that skittered down his spine. Women with plans usually meant trouble.

Chapter Seven

The next morning, Eva sat across from Beth at the kitchen table, her breakfast forgotten. She was too excited to eat. She'd sketched out a rough plan of action to become Adam's partner. It was going to take work, much convincing and a solid business plan. But she knew she could do it.

After bouncing the idea off of Beth, Eva leaned back in her chair. "So, what do you think?"

"How much will something like that cost?"

Eva shrugged. "I don't know, but I own the house free and clear. If I can get an appraisal done, I'll know how much I have to work with."

"You'll drain the equity from this house to buy into the orchard? What about your bed-and-breakfast? All that time you invested redoing the rooms." Beth didn't look pleased.

Eva knew her parents wouldn't be happy either. "An ownership interest in the orchard will help the

B and B. I need those cherry trees, Beth. People will come to my place versus somewhere else because of the novelty of staying on a working cherry farm."

Beth didn't look convinced. "You've got this all figured out."

Eva nodded.

Beth tapped the tip of her butter knife on the edge of her plate. "Managing the orchard isn't enough."

"No." Eva sat straighter. "Marsh Orchards could have been so much more than it was. I wanted to make it more, but then Dad sold it. Besides, there's nothing to stop Adam from selling to a developer or mowing down the trees himself to build summer homes for his family."

Beth gave her a long look. "What makes you think he'll do that?"

Eva took a deep breath. She couldn't explain the dread that filled her when Adam's sister pointed out *her* perfect building site. Before they left last night, Adam told Eva that he'd be bringing his father by later today to see the farm. More unpleasant possibilities were bound to surface.

"Don't you see? Adam can do anything he wants with the land. He owns it, he decides. But if I were his partner, I'd have a say on part of it. Hopefully the part closest to the house."

Beth's eyes narrowed. "Are you sure this is about the farm?"

Eva snapped her head up. "What do you mean?"

"I see the way you and Adam look at each other. Are you hoping a partnership might keep him here?"

"Not at all." Eva shook her head, but her voice lacked conviction. Adam was part of the draw, too. He was used to beautiful, cultured women and by all appearances he'd never been seriously involved with any of them. Why would she be any different?

Eva wanted to keep this professional. She didn't want to be discarded after a few dates. After she'd grown to care...

Who was she kidding? She already cared.

Her roommate still didn't look convinced. In fact, Beth laughed. "You're so in denial."

Maybe she was, but she couldn't let her feelings for Adam mess up what had to be done. "I have a lot of planning to do before I can broach the subject. That'll take some time."

"It might not hurt to sweeten him up a little, you know." Beth grinned.

"Beth!" Eva knew the contempt Adam carried for gold diggers. She wasn't after his money, just part of the orchard. But she'd bring value to Adam by helping him turn Marsh Orchards into a retail farm. That was where they'd both find success.

"I'm not saying to romance him into a partnership, but show him what you're capable of. That he'll need you and your business to make his grow."

"Exactly." Eva frowned as it dawned on her. That was easier said than done. A business plan on paper was one thing but… "So, how do I do that?"

"Show you care and why. Let your guard down and maybe he'll do the same. Keep baking for him. I noticed that he asked you to make something for him to go with Uncle Larry's honey. Eva, that's the key. Show him how successful your breakfasts can be."

Eva had been baking for Adam for entirely different reasons, but Beth was onto something. Sweet cherries made a nice retail crop. Something they could share in the results. With Adam's resources and her experience, the possibilities were indeed vast.

All Adam had to do was agree to her offer.

Adam walked along the edge of the orchard with his father. Leonard Peece had meticulously scanned the property and its views in relative silence. He'd ask a question here and there but otherwise frowned at everything Adam showed him.

"There's considerable value in this land. A good investment," his father finally said.

"I know."

"But will your cherry harvest pay for itself?"

Adam shrugged to ease the knot of tension that had settled in the base of his neck. He knew what his father was getting at. He was sick of Adam's *hobbies* that took him away from Peece Canning. "Depends on a lot of things. Weather, pests, demand."

His father shook his head. "Too much risk. At least the land has potential if you go belly-up."

Failure wasn't an option. Not this time. Adam had felt a connection with this property the moment he'd laid eyes on it. Like a calling from God, Adam needed to keep it and work it. He had to succeed. Adam looked up in time to see Eva approach. She was part of the reason he couldn't fail. He didn't want to let her down.

She looked uneasy when she glanced at his father. "Hi, I'm Eva. I have coffee and homemade donuts at the house if you're interested."

"I've seen everything I need to see," his father said with a broad grin. "Donuts, did you say?"

"Eva, this is my father, Leonard Peece."

She held out her hand. "Mr. Peece."

Adam watched his father take an assessing look at Eva before he clasped her hands between his own. "Now I understand my son's fascination with farming."

Eva glanced his way before addressing his father. "Growing cherries is hard work, Mr. Peece. But satisfying."

She hadn't missed his father's implication, but she didn't react to it. Adam knew his father's perspective—farming couldn't be the only reason

Adam had for walking away from Peece Canning. A woman, however, made more sense.

"Of course it is." His dad gave Eva a wink. "Especially surrounded by such beauty."

Eva's cheeks colored, but instead of shying away she met his father's gaze with a smile. "I wouldn't be anywhere else."

His father took her arm in his, effectively blocking Adam out as they made their way to the house. "Now, tell me about this land."

"Well, it's been in my family for eighty some odd years. My great-grandfather was the first to farm it."

"And my son here, he's an outsider. Do you think he's up to continuing the tradition?"

Adam shook his head. His father was testing him through her, trying to gauge his commitment by her answers.

Eva glanced back at him with a glint of mischief in her eyes. "He's a good worker, but I'm not convinced he can connect with this land without a Marsh to help him."

His father laughed. "Well put."

And Adam watched his father succumb to yet another female. Eva had charmed Leonard Peece like a pro. What shocked Adam was the warmth that spread through him at Eva's comment. He didn't expect to *like* needing her.

They stepped into Eva's kitchen and the divine

smell of melted chocolate and brewed coffee had Adam's mouth watering. "Wow, Eva."

Her cheeks turned that rosy shade he liked. "They taste even better. Have a seat," she said.

Adam sat across from his father at the long kitchen table. A coffee service had been set between them bed-and-breakfast style. Floral plates and cups arranged next to a pretty platter of cake donuts glazed with chocolate. Impressive.

"Dig in," Eva said as she scooted into the chair next to him.

Adam grabbed a chocolate-cherry donut. They were still warm. He bit into bliss. "These are... wow."

Eva tipped her head in acknowledgment. "Thank you."

Adam's father had been a little too quiet. But Adam realized his dad was busy enjoying the baked confection that was too good for words. "Pretty good, huh?"

His father patted Eva's hand resting on the table. "You could make a killing with these. My dear, what are you doing working for my son? You should be working for me. I'm glad you're joining us for dinner. Maybe we can chat about that."

Eva laughed. "Thank you, but I hope to open my home as a bed-and-breakfast. Having a working cherry orchard right next door with incredible views will bring the guests, but these—" Eva raised her donut. "These will keep them coming back."

Adam watched his father digest that bit of news with a sharp look his way. Adam hadn't told his dad about Eva's plans. Leonard Peece might actually take his son's efforts more seriously now that someone else's dreams depended on Adam's success.

That evening, Eva and Beth pulled into the driveway of the Peece family's town house right behind Adam's Jeep. A black Mercedes Benz was parked in the left open bay of a three-car garage.

"Whoa. This is nice," Beth said. "Adam's got it going on."

"Wait till you meet his dad." Eva knew where Adam's allure came from. His father had a magnetic personality mixed with distinguished good looks, compliments of his Italian ancestry. It explained his appeal to women regardless of age. Leonard might be handsome, but he was genuine, too. Despite his implied doubt with Adam's farming venture, Eva sensed a vein of pride in his son.

Eva knocked on the front door.

The door opened to reveal a girl around the age of four wearing a pink tutu. Her eyes were big green marbles framed by a mop of dark brown curls. "Hello?"

Eva's heart melted. "Hello. My name's Eva and this is Beth. We're friends of Adam. Can we come in?"

Adam appeared behind the little girl, dragging a smaller version on his leg. "Let them in, Cinda."

Suddenly shy, Cinda ran away and hid behind Adam's free leg.

Seeing two little girls hanging all over Adam made Eva smile. "Babysitting?"

"No, everyone's here. Come on in." After Adam closed the door, he asked, "Where's Ryan?"

"He decided not to come. He's tied up in a building project." Eva smiled at the two-year-old clamped onto Adam's leg, using his foot as a seat. She drooled all over his jeans. "Hello there."

"His house on the lake? Yeah, he mentioned that he was restoring it." Adam lifted his burdened leg to the squealed laughter of both girls. "This little one is Bella."

"Adam showed us how to color." Cinda had come out from hiding.

Beth immediately knelt down. "Do you like to color?"

The girl nodded and came out a little more.

Eva grinned at Adam. "You're such the ladies' man."

"I can't seem to get rid of them." He scooped Bella up and threw her in the air to more screeching delight and giggles when he caught her.

"Me next, Adam." Cinda raised her arms.

Anne met them in the foyer. "Eva, Beth, let me take your jackets. Dinner's in a few minutes, but please come in and sit down. And forgive Adam's terrible manners."

"I have my hands full," Adam said as he repeated the toss and catch with Cinda. Another peal of little-girl laughter.

"No Ryan?" Anne gestured for them to follow.

"Not this time." Eva stepped forward, but she couldn't tear her gaze away from Adam playing with his two half sisters. It was more than the roughhousing any big brother would do. Adam was a natural with kids.

Anne took charge. "Girls, go wash your hands. We're going to eat."

The toddlers didn't look as if they'd comply. Then Adam made a growling sound and crouched like a bear ready to chase them. Off they went, screaming down the hall into the bathroom.

"Cute kids," Beth said.

Anne rolled her eyes. "Noisy and a little spoiled, but we love them. Come on, I'll get you ladies something to drink."

And so began the evening in the Peece household. Anne introduced them to Leonard's lovely young wife, Heather, who bustled about the kitchen beside her husband. Enough shrimp and chicken to feed an army sizzled on their stovetop grill. And Eva felt oddly at home.

When everyone was finally seated around the table laden with steaming food, the high-chair-restrained toddlers pounded their spoons.

"Girls! That's enough," their mother admonished, and the banging stopped.

Heather wasn't what Eva had expected. She was pretty with the same green eyes as the girls, but her hair was more red than brown, and her figure was more lush than lean. Not a painted long fingernail or fake eyelash in sight. Heather looked like any young mother of two.

Eva glanced at Adam, and he gave her a wink that made her heart flip. She couldn't shake the image of him with Bella and Cinda. Too easily, she imagined Adam holding a child of theirs with blue eyes and freckles across the nose. A deep yearning pierced low in her belly.

"My father says you make donuts worth marketing," Anne said.

"That's right." Eva bit into her chicken and glanced at Adam. The muscle in his jaw tightened. Maybe his father wasn't kidding about that job.

"I've got a marketing degree, so if you need any advertising help with your B and B, give me a call," Anne continued.

"Thanks." Eva wanted to set them all straight.

"I'd never leave my home, or Northern Michigan for that matter."

"That orchard means a lot to you, doesn't it?" Leonard Peece joined the conversation.

Tension swelled around her, emanating from Adam to his father and even Anne looked uncomfortable. It felt as if there was something unknown riding on her answer.

She glanced at Adam, but he wouldn't look at her. With a deep breath, she decided on honesty. "I've loved that land all my life. I'm glad for the opportunity to work it."

At that moment, Bella threw a stray noodle that bounced off her father's nose. Everyone laughed and the tension was broken. But Eva felt as if she'd missed something important.

The next morning Eva entered church after her usual sweep of the area looking for Todd before she stepped into the sanctuary. With the coast clear, Eva slipped into their fourth-row pew.

Adam was there with his sister.

"Morning," she said.

He looked up. "Hey."

By now Eva was used to seeing Adam in church on Sunday, but this morning's look from him knocked her off kilter. "Where's your dad?"

"He's not much of a churchgoer," Anne said.

"Dad and Heather are packing up the girls to go home."

"Oh." Eva sat next to Adam.

"Annie's staying a couple more days," Adam explained.

His sister smiled. "I want to hit the shops in Leland, and I'm dying to see *Fishtown*. Would you and Beth like to join me? We could do lunch on me."

Did the Peece family think they could buy everything? Eva didn't need someone picking up her tab. Still, she couldn't remember the last time she'd been shopping for the fun of it and Leland was only a stone's throw away. "Beth spends Sunday afternoons with her mom. But I'll have to check—"

"Please say yes. Adam wants to work on the farm equipment so my afternoon is totally open."

Eva glanced at Adam. "Anything wrong?"

Adam shook his head. "Ryan's going to show me how to hook up the attachments to the tractors, so that's one less thing to do tomorrow before we fertilize. We might even break out the ATVs."

It shouldn't irritate her that Ryan had stepped into her role. She might not be a fan of messing with the equipment, but it was her job. And Adam was *her* boss. Why hadn't he asked her? Unless her brother offered, but still… "Do you need my help?"

"I got it. Besides, Sundays are your days off. Go have fun."

Eva clenched her jaw. She didn't like the feeling that working with Adam might be more fun than shopping with Anne. Nope, she had to go. She needed a break. It couldn't be good to want to spend every day with one's boss.

Eva's curiosity with Adam had been piqued even more after having dinner with his family last night. She faced his sister. "I could use a girls' day out. I'll go, Anne."

"Great, we can head out after service." His sister wore a satisfied smile, and Eva got the distinct feeling that Anne was just as curious about her, too.

The song service started, cutting off further discussion. Once seated for the message, Eva fidgeted more than she listened. She'd gotten out of the habit of bringing her Bible to church because she hardly read it. That stab of shame wasn't something to be proud of. She glanced at God's word lying open flat across Adam's lap.

"You can look on with me." He scooted closer and his thigh brushed hers.

She twitched but otherwise recovered.

"Too much coffee this morning?" he whispered.

"No, why?"

"You're a little jumpy," he teased.

Pathetic was more like it when it came to the effect Adam's nearness had on her. She couldn't slide away from him without broadcasting that fact, so she did her best to ignore it.

While the minister delivered his sermon and they thumbed through various passages, Eva was blown away by the writing and underlines in Adam's Bible. "Is this yours?"

"What?"

"The Bible. Is it yours?" she whispered.

"Who else's would it be?"

She ran her finger across a page with highlighted passages and notes written along the margin. "What's with the scribbles?"

She felt him shift next to her. "I like to study."

Wow. Adam's commitment to learning God's Word pricked her spirit. Her dried-up and neglected spirit. She used to tackle the scriptures with vigor, seeking answers to so many questions and jotting down thoughts in her journal.

"Why not use a notebook?"

He shrugged. "I might lose it."

He wouldn't lose his Bible, though. From the look of the dog-eared corners of several pages, he was a frequent reader. She admired him for that.

"You really have left behind what you used to be." The comment slipped from her lips before she'd thought it through. Before she realized it gave a little of herself away, too. Where Adam had found faith, Eva had lost hers.

He looked at her closely. "For the first time in a long while there's purpose to my life. I'm finding out what I really want."

Eva couldn't claim the same satisfaction. Some days she felt far removed from the girl she used to be. Everything she'd ever wanted was gone. Her family scattered except for her and Ryan.

Trust didn't come easily. Not after Todd. She was scared to let herself fall for a guy like Adam. Even more afraid of letting him get too close. She'd had her fill of heartbreak. And everything she knew about Adam screamed a broken heart waiting to happen.

After church, Eva went shopping with Anne, then to lunch. Once seated and served, Eva gathered her courage enough to ask, "What did your father think of the orchard?"

"Very impressed with the land. He thought it was beautiful and a good investment." Anne took a quick sip of her water.

Not the answer Eva hoped for. "And the farm. Does he think your brother has what it takes to become a grower?"

Anne laughed. "That's hard to tell. Adam's never been one to stay with something or someone for very long. Even at Peece Canning. He says he likes hands-on work, but he spent only a year overseeing the canning plants. Although he sure liked driving those forklifts."

Eva smiled despite the heaviness that settled in her heart. Adam never stayed with anyone for very long… Eva could only hope for a strong professional relationship with Adam. A friendship was the safest choice. But she could see Adam goofing around on company time. When the company belongs to your family, who wouldn't? "Overseeing a large operation isn't really hands-on."

Anne looked thoughtful a moment. "Yeah, I guess you're right. He's never stopped fiddling with his motorcycles and Dad's antique Corvette since he was a teenager. He still skis, so I guess he's kept up with those things."

Encouraged, Eva probed further. "But Adam likes cherry farming so far, right?"

Adam's sister gave her a shrewd look. "You're hoping he'll stay."

Eva nodded. She didn't like the alternatives that might mean development or a resale. "I think we can help grow each other's businesses in time."

"Well, I don't know how much time Adam has to decide. He bought your farm by borrowing against his share of Peece Canning. I imagine that note will come due sometime soon and then he'll have to choose."

Any effort to positively spin Adam's intentions was pointless. Even if he wanted to remain a grower, what if it was financially not feasible? Where would that leave Eva? Even more determined, Eva knew she had to become Adam's partner for the benefit of her bed-and-breakfast.

Eva prayed Adam would choose Marsh Orchards. That was far more important than a relationship between them. The orchard had to come first.

For now, anyway.

Chapter Eight

A couple of days later, Adam watched Eva's expression morph from disbelief to gall mixed with confusion.

"You did what?"

He opened the side door of the pole barn. "I ordered turkey manure. It'll be delivered today."

"Why?"

He figured his reason was pretty clear, but he'd spell it out if he had to. "For fertilizer."

"But we have fertilizer. We've been applying it for two days."

"This is more natural." And he needed every possible edge he could get.

She shook her head. "That stuff's going to stink. We have neighbors, you know."

Adam opened the main doors and peeked outside. "Where? Our nearest neighbor is like a mile or more away."

Eva gave a sardonic laugh. "Don't worry, that smell will travel."

Adam considered the grim line of her lips. Miss Prickly Prim had him there. "So it'll smell bad for a couple days, maybe even a week. This *is* farmland. Besides, I checked."

Her eyes widened. "With who?"

Eva looked incredibly pretty this morning with her hair pulled back into a ponytail that swished every time she made her point. It almost cost him his argument.

"Jim Sanborn. He's been using poultry manure for a few years now and said it makes a huge difference in the health of the trees."

She couldn't knock Jim's advice and he could tell it galled her. Jim was a seasoned fruit farmer with a solid reputation and a lifetime local. "But we already have the nitrogen fertilizer. Can you cancel yours?"

"I'm not going to. I want to try this." He glanced back at her, wondering if she'd ever be as sweet on him as her cherries.

Her cheeks turned rosy, and she took a step back. "You're spending double needlessly. And you're taking a big chance of irritating our neighbors."

"I'm sure they'll get over it. There isn't a smell ordinance in this county, is there?"

"No, but…"

He waited with a cocked eyebrow for her to continue.

Instead she sputtered, "You're impossible."

Adam understood where she was coming from. Eva was his farm manager, and this was a discussion he should have had with her before ordering. He used to hate it when his father made changes to his presentations without giving him a heads-up. But Adam didn't want to leave anything to chance. Doing something the way it had always been done wasn't the way he'd make it.

Eva stopped what she was doing and asked, "How are you going to apply the manure? We don't have a spreader."

"Yeah, we do."

She faced him. "Since when?"

"Since your father sold it to me. It's old, he said he didn't use it anymore, but it works. Ryan showed me how to hook it up."

She pursed her lips into that stubborn line he was beginning to recognize as Eva struggling for control. He waited, imagining all kinds of words flitting through her brain begging to be born, but none came.

Instead, she agreed. "We'll spread the manure. But next time Ryan helps you with a grand idea, do you think you could let me in on it, too?"

He couldn't blame her for being a little sore. But the way she'd voiced her opinion without pushing for her way only made him admire her more. "Understood. I'm not sure if I ordered enough, so we'll still use the nitrogen. We can donate any unopened fertilizer to the research center."

She gave him a nod. "And then we'll see if it makes a difference. It's your dime, Peece."

Another challenge. It might be his money, but her pride was on the line. He had no intention of squandering either one, even if he knew he was right. He had to be.

After a week spent applying two different fertilizers a few feet from the base of the trees, the weather cooperated perfectly by giving them a couple days of soft spring rain to soak up the sharp smell of poultry manure. The days that followed were filled with sunny warmth, giving Eva hope that the cherry buds would soon start to pop.

Staring out of the barn while Adam prepped the tractors for a day of spraying the field, Eva hoped all this work wouldn't go to waste. What if Adam chose to return to Peece Canning?

Adam waved his hand in front of her face. "You in there, Eva?"

"Yeah." She blinked, returning her focus to the early-morning fog that had settled in the valley. The barn doors were open to the view she'd grown up loving. She didn't want to see it changed. Or lost.

"You were miles away just now."

Eva shook off her thoughts. "Did you know that your sister sent me a note thanking me for shopping with her? I should be the one sending her a thank-you for picking up lunch."

Adam chuckled. "She's proper that way. She had a great time with you. Not surprising since you're the kind of girl she needs to hang around."

Eva cocked her head. "Why's that?"

"You're not prissy like a lot of her friends. Anne could use some earthy influence."

"I'm earthy?" Eva had never been described that way.

He lifted both of her hands and flipped them palm up. "You've got dirt on your fingers and turkey poo on your boots. Yeah, I'd say you are."

"A girl doesn't grow up hoping to be called *earthy,* you know." Eva knew she wasn't polished or cultured. Not like Anne, who was the director of marketing for Peece Canning Corporation. She had an MBA and had been all over the world like her brother.

Adam kneaded her palms with his thumbs. "What if I think *earthy* is beautiful?"

Eva didn't have an answer for him because her heart had just leaped into her throat, making speech impossible. Dragging her attention from their clasped hands, she looked into his eyes and got sucked in. The soft pressure of his massaging touch kept her from looking away, let alone pulling her hands back.

"You smell good." His voice was low and richer than cream.

She had to put a stop to this before she melted into a puddle at his feet. Letting out a bark of laughter, Eva pulled free. "I can't believe you can smell anything over your *natural* fertilizer."

Adam watched her climb into the cockpit of the smaller tractor. The stench in parts of the field was strong but not in the barn. Not when he stood close to her.

He rubbed the back of his neck. He had no business doing that, but it was getting difficult to keep his distance. Adam was definitely infatuated with his farm manager.

Not unexpected, considering that he fell into attraction pretty easily. Remaining interested after getting involved proved the tough part. Falling in love might as well be a foreign language. He didn't understand it, but maybe it was time to learn. Eva might make the perfect teacher for him. Hauling himself up into the larger John Deere, Adam put away thoughts of romancing Miss Prickly Prim. He had a job to do first.

After hours spent in the field, rain clouds rolled in and the wind picked up, making the raindrops hit the tractor cockpit like kicked-up pebbles. His cell phone rang. It was Eva.

"Yeah?"

"We might as well call it a day and finish up tomorrow. Spraying's not going to work in this wind."

"Meet you back at the barn." Adam ended the call and slipped his phone in his pocket.

The afternoon was shot, but Adam didn't want to go home. He'd organize the farm files that Bob Marsh had left behind and call him with any questions.

He'd like to ask Eva out but knew better. Dating her was risky until after July when the harvest was in and success was certain. Could he hold out that long?

Once back in the barn, Eva leaped from her tractor and bounded toward him with a broad grin. "Did you see those buds?"

Blinded by the brightness of her expression and the sweetness of her smile, he couldn't recall. He was lucky to remember to cut the engine on his tractor. "Ah, yeah."

Eva laughed. "Okay, I know they're small, but they're there. We'll have blossoms the first week of May at this rate."

Her excitement was contagious. The fire in her eyes confirmed her passion for the orchard. Each year she'd seen the turning of nature and yet it still inspired her. She inspired him.

He slid out of the tractor's cockpit. "May's when you bring in the bees, right?"

She laughed again. "Uh-huh. I love bee time. Uncle Larry delivers the hives. We place them in the orchard and the bees do their thing for about a week or so. We get sweet cherries and honey. God knew what He was doing, didn't He?"

"Definitely," Adam said, enraptured.

Her eyes narrowed as if she'd suddenly realized he wasn't quite keeping up. Or maybe he was staring at her like an idiot. "Ah, yeah. I have an appointment with my bank at four. Do you mind if I get a head start and leave now?"

He didn't like the pinch of disappointment he felt at her leaving. "Go ahead. I'll take care of cleanup."

"Thanks, Peece. See you tomorrow." Eva practically ran from the barn.

She was awfully animated for a trip to the bank. Her meeting had to be about the financing for her bed-and-breakfast. Their recent conversations had been filled with the various spray applications needed before the leaves unfurled. If she got her loan and business up and running, how long could she stay on as his farm manager? Their contract covered only this season.

After going through the farm files and giving Bob Marsh an update over the phone, Adam locked the pole barn for the night. He climbed into his Jeep and headed home. He couldn't help but wonder what it would be like to have someone waiting for him. Someone he could share his dreams with and build something that might last.

Was that even possible anymore?

Was it possible for him?

True to Eva's word, less than two weeks later the month of May brought blossoms and bees. Adam watched her uncle Larry gingerly douse the stacked beehives with smoke to keep them inside their wooden homes. Larry checked every box hive loaded on the flatbed truck with loving care after the five-mile trek from their place.

Adam slipped his hands into the canvas gloves Eva gave him, but he continued to watch her uncle. Bees buzzed around the man as if they knew him. No threat, no swarm. Would the colony accept a stranger like him as gently? Adam had been brought up to stay far away from bees and yet tonight he'd move a bunch of live beehives all over his sweet orchard.

"Here's a windbreaker and net hat. I suggest you wear both." Eva's aunt Jamee nudged his shoulder.

Larry had explained when he signed the bee rental contract that they moved the hives at night, when the bees were settled in and quiet. Tonight promised to be cool with a sky sprinkled with stars, while a half moon made its appearance against the darkening horizon. Adam had dressed as Eva directed—two pairs of socks, long-sleeved shirt and jeans. "I brought a sweatshirt."

"Trust me, you'll want elastic around your wrists and waist. Bees can crawl under sweatshirts."

Adam held out his hand for the gear. He didn't want to test Jamee's do-it-or-you'll-be-sorry grin any more than he wanted a run-in with a bee under his shirt.

"Nervous?" Eva gave him a cheeky grin. She wore a wide-brimmed hat covered with netting that made her look as if she was headed for a garden tea party.

"Should I be?"

"Don't bump or drop a hive. They get upset if jostled." Larry slapped him on the back.

Great. "I'll be gentle."

Eva's uncle winked. "Adam, let me tell you something about bees. In some ways, they're a lot like women. Show respect for their ability, give them love and security, and they'll make sweet honey for you. Skip any of the three, and you'll get stung."

Adam laughed. "I'll remember that."

"See that you do."

Adam caught the warning in Larry's words. Obviously, he didn't want to see his niece getting hurt. Adam didn't either, but good intentions didn't make the warm feelings flooding his heart any easier to ignore.

They began the slow trek into the orchard. Eva's aunt Jamee drove the flatbed at a walking pace while Larry handed down the square beehives for Adam and Eva to place.

The scents of the orchard at night filled Adam's nostrils, a heady mix of cherry blossoms and damp grass. Eva's soft scent mixed in whenever she got close. There were plenty of opportunities for Eva's shoulder to rub against his because they positioned the hives atop wooden pallets right next to each other.

Lifting a hive from the flatbed, Adam caught sight of a bee making its merry way up his arm, and he froze. "Hey, hey, what's he going to do?"

"Careful, Adam. Don't tip the hive," Larry said.

At that moment Adam concentrated on the bee's journey toward his face. They were lucky he didn't dump the hive, let alone care about tipping it.

"Hold still." Eva pressed her gloved hand against Adam's shoulder until the bee walked onto her finger. "They won't hurt you. See?"

Adam watched as she gently coaxed the bee back into the hive's opening. "What if they all come out?"

She took the hive from him, her eyes shining with amusement. "That's the goal. But not tonight."

Larry doused the remaining hives on the truck with smoke to calm them down. Adam had to admit the novelty of tonight's work had worn off. He was tired and not in the mood to get stung. Still, he couldn't help but enjoy watching Eva, who acted like a kid placing presents under a Christmas tree.

"She really loves this, doesn't she?" Adam said to her uncle.

Larry agreed. "Bee time has always been her favorite. Eva's not short on determination, that's for sure. Growing up with two older brothers has a lot to do with it."

Adam suspected her drive grew from something else. Something that also made Eva vulnerable. He'd catch glimpses of that vulnerability every now and then. It made him work that much harder, hoping to protect her from his potential loss.

"Why bees, Larry?"

"Bees have order and follow a system of orders. I started beekeeping as a hobby, but after I retired from the military, I grew it into a business. There are not many of us around here."

Adam nodded. Now he understood Larry's no-nonsense approach and the controlled way the man carried himself. "Where'd you serve?"

"Eighty-second Airborne Division. I wasn't interested in farming like my brother, so I joined the army and made a career out of it. My son has followed my footsteps and is stationed in Afghanistan. But I hope to leave the beekeeping business to him."

"Does he want it?" Adam knew what it was like to disappoint a father's expectations. But Larry's pride in his son's military prowess wouldn't fade no matter what Larry's son did with the bee business. Adam envied the guy.

Larry shrugged. "It's here if and when he wants it."

"Well, if he doesn't want it, keep us in mind." Adam hooked his thumb to include Eva, who'd moved ahead to talk with her aunt.

Larry's eyes narrowed. "Eva's already on the list. She's sharp. My brother was too set in his ways to try some of the things she'd suggested. You couldn't have picked a better manager. Eva knows her cherries, but baking with them is what drives her."

Adam kept his eye on Eva's back. A B and B was the perfect showcase for her freshly baked goods. "I know."

"She's a good girl, the kind you keep."

Adam looked up at Larry, sitting on the side of the flatbed. "I know that, too."

"See that you don't forget." Larry's eyes shimmered with protective intensity.

"Forget what?" Eva came back for a hive.

Larry grinned and handed her a hive. "Where you got your start making pastry by helping your aunt Jamee." He looked at Adam. "My wife's a caterer."

"Eva mentioned that." Adam took a hive, too, nestling it near the one Eva had placed.

Why had Eva chosen a culinary path over agriculture? He wondered if her father had ever considered leaving the farm to Eva. Bob Marsh had been candid about the financial position of Marsh Orchards before he agreed to sell. Bob had been up to his ears in debt just like his father before him. Eva's dad said he didn't want to pass those headaches to his daughter.

But if Bob Marsh's finances had been in better shape, Adam might never have met Eva. Never had the chance to do something he'd always wanted to do. The old saying that God moved in mysterious ways rang true.

Adam let loose a noisy yawn.

"Just a few more and we'll be done," Larry said.

Adam scanned the half-dozen hives still on the flatbed and laughed. "Good to hear."

"What's the matter, Peece? Tired?" Eva rested glove-clad hands on her hips.

Adam's eyelids might as well have been lined with lead. "We put in a full day today."

Fortunately, Eva's brother lived within a few miles and he'd invited Adam to stay over. Adam wouldn't have made the hour-long drive home without falling asleep on his bike. Now that the weather had turned warm, Adam drove his Harley to work. Tomorrow morning, he'd be back to inspect the orchard and make sure the bees were buzzing in and out of the blooms like they were supposed to.

"Today's one of many yet to come," Eva said.

Did she still think he was a city boy playing grower? More than anything he wanted this to work, he wanted to keep the orchard intact. Feeling like someone watched him, Adam glanced at Eva's aunt through the opened window of the truck.

"Eva wants you to do well." Jamee gave him an encouraging wink.

Adam wondered if she expected him to give up, too. "So when's this honey going to be ready?"

"I gave Eva a jar from last year's batch. Make sure she shares it with you," Jamee said.

Adam looked at Eva. "Hey, maybe you can practice your breakfast skills with that honey tomorrow."

"You got it. Breakfast tomorrow morning at nine so we can sleep in a little. Aunt Jamee, you and Uncle Larry are welcome to come." Eva stifled a yawn of her own. "Let Ryan know he can come, too."

"Sounds good." Right now all Adam could think about was his pillow. And how much he liked the warmth of Eva's family. They looked out for each other.

Adam and Anne stuck together, but they were too wrapped up in their own stuff to take care of each other like Eva's family did. In many ways it was the same with their father. Their futures may have been set, but Adam and Anne hadn't been coddled. They came from their father's first family, from the first wife Leonard Peece tried so hard to forget.

Eva's family was yet another attraction for him. If he got involved with Eva only to lose the farm, he'd alienate the whole lot of them. The expertise of her father, who remained a phone call away, and the friendship he'd forged with Ryan. Adam couldn't risk losing those connections.

Oatmeal griddlecakes infused with bananas and dried cherries doused in cherry blossom honey, and a side of link sausages. A hearty meal, but would it work to her advantage in becoming his partner?

Eva, dressed in her standard jeans and a T-shirt, surveyed her work while the coffeemaker chugged. She'd met with her loan officer about a home equity application and it looked promising. She'd also gone to several appointments with a volunteer business group that helped first-timers develop strong business plans. She was almost ready to approach Adam with her proposal.

"Morning." Adam peeked his head in from the porch.

"Come in," she called.

He entered the kitchen dressed for the day's work in the field. He grabbed a coffee mug and helped himself to the pot.

"Where's Ryan?"

"Couldn't make it." He looked around. "Where's your aunt and uncle?"

"They decided to stay home." Eva lifted the lid of her chafing dish filled with hot food. Great, a big breakfast made with only her and Adam to enjoy it. Beth had already left for school. "I hope you're hungry."

Adam peered over her shoulder. "Always. Smells good."

He did, too. His aftershave had a woodsy scent she liked. Rich yet unassuming. A lot like the man who wore it. Before she offered to fix Adam a plate, she noticed that his damp hair looked shorter. She openly stared.

"What?"

"You got a haircut?" Eva couldn't keep the amusement out of her voice when she noticed it wasn't quite up to Adam's style.

Adam's eyes narrowed. "My stylist is downstate, so I went to the barber in town. He butchered it."

"You have a stylist?" Eva's eyes must have bulged with shock considering the sheepish expression that flitted across Adam's face.

"Well, yeah. You don't think this just happens by itself, do you?" He recovered quickly enough and gave her an insolent wink as he took the plate from her hand and filled it with food.

Eva burst out laughing. Her father and brothers had always used the barber in town with no complaints. She'd given them trims in between. She still cut Ryan's hair when he was either too lazy or cheap to make the trip into LeNaro.

She'd never met a guy who went to a salon on purpose. Failing to keep the giggle out of her voice, Eva managed, "I'm sure Beth can give you pointers on who to use when she gets home from school."

"Nice. So, where do you go?"

Eva shrugged. "Wherever. Sometimes, I cut it myself."

He gave her head a quick once-over. "Maybe next time you can cut mine."

She forced herself not to squirm under his intent perusal.

Eva wouldn't mind sinking her fingers in that raven-dark hair of his, but she believed in playing it safe. Cutting Adam's hair promised to be anything but. "I don't think so."

"Why?"

"I'll do it wrong and you'll hate it."

"Chicken." Adam slipped into the chair.

Got that right. Eva didn't voice her thought. She'd been afraid of a lot for too long. But maybe it was time to change that. Starting with Adam.

He lifted the decanter of warmed honey. "Is this it? Cherry blossom honey?"

"It is."

He held it under his nose as if it were a fine wine. "Nice."

"There's maple syrup if you don't like it." Eva watched as he poured the honey over a portion of his stacked pancakes.

He took a bite and nodded. "It's good. Very good."

Eva smiled. "Marketable?"

He looked at her. "For your bed-and-breakfast?"

"Packaged griddlecake mix that guests can buy to take home."

"With a pretty bottle of cherry blossom honey. That'd be a nice touch."

"I think so, too." Eva bit her tongue before she blurted out a partnership offer right then and there. Instead, she filled her plate and sat next to Adam and ate.

Adam had polished off two helpings by the time Eva finished her one. She didn't know where the guy put it. He was slender, wiry even, but he could pack away enough food to rival her brothers.

She could get used to making breakfasts for Adam. Like caring for him when he was ill, the truth of how much she'd grown to care for Adam didn't surprise her. But could she trust him with her heart?

They finished in silence, until Adam picked up their plates and headed for the dishwasher. "I'll clean up."

"Thanks."

Yup, she liked hanging out with Adam in the kitchen. In the field, the barn, church. Eva liked being around him. A good thing considering the long work days ahead. But what about after that? Could she be his reason to stay?

She stashed the leftovers in the fridge and then checked the thermometer on the porch. Sixty-five and only ten o'clock. The weatherman predicted low seventies and sunny. A perfect day for pollination. "Ready to check the bees?"

Adam wiped his hands on a dishtowel. "Sure."

Once outside, Eva tipped her face toward the warm sunshine. Spring was her favorite season. And May was her favorite month because the air smelled sweet and the bees bobbed and weaved in the cherry blossoms.

Walking the orchard lanes filled with newly opened blooms transported her to when she'd been a kid and walked with her dad. It wasn't easy to accept someone other than a Marsh owning such beauty. But she'd change part of that if Adam agreed to her plan.

Despite her distance from God, Eva couldn't help but thank Him this morning and offer up a small petition. *Please, Lord, let this partnership work out somehow.*

"This is amazing. It's like the blossoms burst open overnight." Adam's voice interrupted her silent prayer.

Eva recognized the awe in Adam's voice. His eyes held the same unbridled pride as her father's when they'd take this walk. Checking blossoms and bees. It didn't get much better. "I know."

Their steps slowed and Eva reached out for a branch of a nearby tree. Holding a blossom between her fingers, she gestured for Adam to come close. "This is what we're looking for. Nice healthy blooms with no evidence of damage from bugs or rot."

He stood close enough behind her that she felt the warmth from his body. "I see."

She fought the sudden urge to lean into him. For a moment they both stood still, pretending to study the bloom, but Eva knew better. If Adam felt the same pull between them as she did, then he was soaking up the closeness, too. Would he do something about it? Would she?

"Come on. There are more blooms to check." Her voice came out a ragged whisper.

Adam followed Eva all over the sweet cherry orchard. They checked the trees, the opened blooms and closed ones. They watched bees flying from one blossom to the next doing their thing. The morning was quiet but busy with the perpetuation of life. The

Eden-like setting combined with the knowledge that birds and bees were pairing up heightened the draw he already felt toward Eva.

It didn't get more basic than walking through paradise with a woman named Eva. She seemed so right for him. But what did he know? He didn't have a track record with commitment. He didn't have a good example to follow either.

He'd catch Eva watching him, as if she might be thinking the same kind of things. But as soon as he nudged close, she'd shy away.

They walked deeper into the back fifteen acres of mature sweets and checked on the hives. Bees came and went in a flurry of activity. There were so many flying around that Adam waved away a couple buzzing near his head.

"Keep swatting and you'll make them mad," Eva said.

He ducked. "That one dive-bombed me."

"They're honeybees. They don't dive-bomb."

"Ow!" He slapped at his neck, swiping away a bee. "Oh, no? I just got stung."

Eva rushed forward and flipped over the dead insect lying on the ground. "You killed one of Uncle Larry's bees! If you'd have stopped flailing, he would have gone on his way."

"They were all over me."

She stepped toward him. "I counted only two."

Adam scratched his sore neck.

"Let me see." She stood on tiptoe.

Adam never thought himself tall. At five foot nine, he was barely considered average height, but Eva was petite. He leaned forward so she could see where the bee had left its stinger. "Do you see it?"

Her fingers prodded his skin. "Tiny, tiny, tiny things. Wait, hold still."

He liked the way she bit her bottom lip when she concentrated.

"Got it. See?" She showed him the stinger before brushing it from her fingertip. "All better."

It wasn't though. His neck ached. "It still hurts."

"You're such a baby." Eva bent down and scooped up some soil.

He watched her spit into the dirt and then stir it in her palm until she formed a paste. He had to ask. "What are you doing?"

"I'm going to make it all better. This mud will help with the swelling."

He laughed. "Whoa, hold on a minute. I was hoping for a simple kiss to make it all better."

Her eyes widened with surprise, and then she laughed. "What are you, nine?"

He stepped closer, curious. "Sometimes."

She hesitated, but Adam saw the spark of interest in her eyes. She considered kissing him. She even looked like she might welcome it. "The mud will do a better job."

"Why don't we try both and then let me decide."

"Because mud's the best bet." She wiped the dirt paste on his neck.

Adam couldn't decide if he should be relieved or disappointed. But he doubted one kiss would be nearly enough. And that'd put him right where he shouldn't go.

Eva stared at Adam and tried to fill in the blanks. She expected that she'd want to kiss Adam Peece. What startled her was how *badly* she wanted to. Thank goodness she'd remembered the spit and dirt remedy she'd learned from her dad. It had given her an out and much-needed space.

"So how long do I have to keep this mud on my neck?"

"Till it dries."

"Nice."

She giggled. "Come on, Peece. We might as well check the tart cherries, too. Their blooms should be close to opening."

"They bloom later?"

She glanced at his neck. He was already brushing the caked-on mud away.

"Usually a week later, sometimes less, sometimes more." Eva breathed a sigh of relief when Adam slipped back into his normal role. Adam was still her boss.

Now that he was a man of faith he wouldn't toy with her affections, but that didn't mean he wanted something permanent either. And right now Eva wanted that partnership more than she wanted a boyfriend. At least, she should.

Not watching where she was walking, she tripped over an exposed tree root and fell forward. Adam caught her arm and tugged her toward him. She landed against his chest. A surprisingly rock-hard mass of muscle for a former paper pusher.

"You okay?" He smiled.

She licked her lips. "Yeah."

His gaze turned intent, and his head moved closer to hers.

Eva knew what was coming. He'd kiss her if she didn't do something. She'd kiss him back if she didn't do something. And that'd ruin everything.

She took a deep breath and said, "I want to be your partner."

He reared his head back with wide eyes. "My what?"

The look of dismay on his face almost made her laugh until she realized that his reaction confirmed that any hint of marriage shot fear into Adam Peece. If that wasn't proof positive that he wasn't interested in anything long-term or lasting, she fooled herself.

But he hadn't let her go. She felt the warmth of

his hands on her back through the cotton fabric of her shirt.

Eva quickly clarified her intent. "Your *business* partner."

Wariness crept into his eyes. "Why?"

"We can help each other build the business shared by both of us eventually. Plus, I'd like a say in the orchard." She shook off the temptation to wrap her arms around Adam's neck. It wasn't easy keeping up a logical conversation when wrapped in such a pleasant embrace.

"You have lots of say. You're my farm manager."

Eva's palms lay flat against Adam's sweatshirt-covered chest. She felt the erratic beating of his heart that thumped in time with her own.

She gave him a gentle shove. "For now maybe, but what if you decide that you don't like cherry farming? There's a lot of risk involved with commercial growing."

He let her go, as if realizing that he still held her. Or maybe her words had put him off. "Trust me, I like it."

She wished she could. "Now maybe, but what happens when you have to pay off your note?"

"How'd you know about that?" His eyes narrowed.

"Your sister told me when we were shopping. She's worried about what you'll do when forced to choose between Marsh Orchards and Peece Canning. When you have to sell your shares."

Adam dropped his head back and stared at the sky. "Eva—"

"Look, I know I'm rushing this, but I'm waiting for the final approval on my equity loan in order to make you an official offer. I have a ton of ideas how to make this orchard more profitable. You don't have to give me your answer now."

"I thought you wanted to finance your bed-and-breakfast?"

"It all goes together, don't you see? You succeed and so do I. My B and B will bring guests to buy your cherries."

She watched him take a deep breath and hold it. Then he let it out with a whoosh. "It doesn't matter what kind of loan you get, Eva. My answer is no."

She expected him to say that. Of course, he'd refuse at first. "Won't you at least think about it?"

He flashed her a wicked smile. "We should get to know each other a whole lot better before making that kind of commitment, don't you think?"

Eva's mouth dropped open. He meant business, didn't he?

Chapter Nine

Beth dropped the newspaper to her lap. "Why'd you tell Adam you wanted to be his business partner? I thought you weren't ready yet."

"I had to." Eva hit the mute button on the remote to silence the evening's newscast. Turning to face Beth sitting at the other end of the couch, Eva needed to unload, to vent—something.

Beth sat up straight, and her eyes gleamed with interest. "Why?"

"Today in the field, Adam tried to kiss me." The memory of it sent a shiver up Eva's spine.

Beth laughed. "And you didn't let him?"

Eva tipped her head back and stared at the ceiling. "I couldn't."

"Why not?" Beth's voice lilted with disbelief. And then she touched her arm. "Scared?"

Eva looked at her friend, the only person in the world who understood her issues. Eva was scared of a lot of things when it came to Adam Peece, but oddly enough, kissing him wasn't one of them. "I wanted to. But if I did, I might have blown any chance of becoming his partner."

"How do you know that?"

Eva thought about the comments Adam had made about his stepmothers, and friends taking advantage. There was little doubt in her mind that if they became romantically involved, Adam would never agree to share ownership of the farm. He'd think she was using him to get to the orchard. "I just do."

Beth's eyes narrowed. "Maybe you're falling for this guy."

Eva's stomach flipped, confirming there was a whole lot more to her feelings than an inconvenient attraction.

"Eva…?" Beth gave her a look, clearly interpreting her hesitation as agreement.

"I like him Beth, I really do, but I'm not sure I can trust him."

She patted her hand. "So what did he say when you made him your offer?"

"He turned me down, which I expected." Eva wasn't about to share Adam's comment about getting to know each other better. That was definitely a mixed signal and Beth would jump all over it.

"Then you've got time to get your plan of action

in order. He knows what you want, so all you have to do is show him that this is what he'll want, too."

Eva's breath hitched at the implications. Did her roommate do that on purpose? She was talking business, right?

Eva didn't need to worry about how to act normal around Adam after today but she would. "You'd think so, but…"

"But what?"

Eva shrugged.

"Have you prayed about this?"

Again Eva shrugged. "Sort of."

Beth sighed. "Eva, what happened to you isn't God's fault."

"I know." But knowing and accepting were two different things.

"The way I see it, you've built up walls to protect yourself, and Adam's circling your fortress. That's why it's so scary. Adam's not the kind of guy a girl refuses."

And that was what troubled her. How could she trust Adam with her heart when he had so many other options? Sure, he'd made positive, faith-filled changes in his life, but that didn't mean he couldn't have his choice of women. Stylish, cultured, beautiful women. She'd be crazy to think he'd settle for her—a cherry farmer who could bake. Big deal. Real exciting stuff for a man who'd been all over the world.

She heard the crunch of gravel in the driveway and got up from the couch. Peeking out the window, Eva saw Ryan exit his truck. Her heart sank when she recognized the wiry build belonging to Adam slip out of the passenger side. She watched him walk toward the porch with the lithe grace of a skier. Yeah, she could fall for him. Easy. But that didn't mean it'd be wise.

Ryan entered the kitchen as Eva dropped the living-room curtains back into place. "Eva? You around?"

"I'm in here." Her voice cracked.

Her brother leaned through the entryway. "Hey, Beth. Eva, do you mind if we clean up here? I've got a temporary water problem at my house."

She stared at Ryan. "Water problem?"

Adam laughed. "He cut through a main pipe."

Eva followed the men back into the kitchen. "Okay, sure. There are towels in the linen closet."

Ryan went straight to the fridge. "Adam can take his first."

"There are two showers upstairs, Ryan."

"I know, but I'm hungry. Got anything good to eat?"

"Leftover pasta and sauce." But Eva didn't look away from Adam.

He didn't look away from her either.

What was he thinking? This morning they'd walked the orchard. And now Adam walked the property lines of her heart and she couldn't say it was a good thing. Circling her fortress, Beth had said. That was exactly the image Eva got as she stared into Adam's eyes. He'd make a handsome knight with all that dark hair and bright blue eyes. What would happen if she let down her drawbridge?

Ryan pulled out several plastic containers. "Wait, what is all this stuff?"

"That's mine." Beth grabbed her container of Chinese food and the two of them jostled each other for first dibs with the microwave.

Adam finally appeared to get his bearings. "I'll be back in a bit."

After he left, Eva turned toward Ryan. "So what's up? Why do you both have to clean up? Where are you going?"

"To a meeting." Ryan scooped out leftover pasta into a bowl and then he poured himself a glass of milk.

Eva felt her eyebrows rise. "There are no IPM meetings scheduled."

"It's at the research center. I've got a new boss. I have to introduce her tonight at the annual think-tank meeting."

"Her?" Eva grinned.

Ryan rolled his eyes. "Yeah. Don't rub it in."

"I didn't say anything." Eva raised her hands in innocence.

"But you're thinking it."

She exchanged a glance with Beth, who pulled her leftovers from the microwave without a word. "So, why is Adam going?"

"We're reviewing this year's cherry trials and I thought that'd be helpful to him. Some big guns will be there with updates from last year—the university dudes, marketers, processors and large commercial growers. More of a meet and greet."

She should be glad that Adam sought out additional resources, but she felt a twinge of exclusion. "Should I go?"

"Not unless you want to," Ryan said

Eva had never liked mingling and she wasn't good at schmoozing. "Nah. I think I'll pass."

Adam unplugged the blow dryer and hung it back in the closet. He ran his fingers through his hair, turning his head this way and that. Definitely shorter than he was used to. His ears showed. So much for the LeNaro barbershop. But with a little product that he didn't have with him, his haircut might work out fine.

He scooped up his dirty clothes and threw them in his duffel. Then he grabbed his towel and headed downstairs.

On his way down, Eva tripped her way up and stopped three steps below him.

He lifted the towel. "Where you do want this?"

"Laundry room."

"Thanks for letting me clean up here."

"No problem."

He moved down a step closer to her. "Today, you said you had a bunch of ideas on how to make the orchard more profitable. I'd like to hear them."

"Now?"

"Not now. Maybe over dinner this weekend?" He'd been thinking about that near-kiss all afternoon.

She scrunched up her nose. "I don't know."

Adam knew by the nervous look on her face that he'd have to do some convincing. "Why not dinner? It's where business is conducted."

Her face suddenly lit up. "How about we go to the sandwich shop in town after church?"

Not quite what he'd been hoping for, but it was a start. A nice, slow start. That was probably better anyway. "If it's nice we could go for a picnic. We can take my bike."

"Your bike?" Her expression looked cautious.

He grinned at her. "My Harley. It's a Softail and one sweet ride."

Panic flickered in her eyes. "I'm not a big fan of motorcycles."

"Come on, Eva, you drive an ATV all over the orchard, so don't tell me you're scared of a motorcycle. On these back roads there's nothing to worry about. I'm careful. You think I'd want to hurt such a pretty face?"

Her lips curved into a smile. "I don't see any scars on yours."

He laughed. "Exactly. So how about it?"

"What if it rains?"

"You worry about everything, don't you? If it's raining, I'll drive my Jeep or we can take your truck. Whatever makes you more comfortable."

He watched her process this new challenge, weighing her options with more than a hint of interest. She wanted to go.

"Pick me up Sunday morning for church with your bike."

"Deal." They stood on the stairs a moment too long, neither one making a move to leave.

"You better get going or you'll be late for your meeting. Ryan's already showered and antsy. I think he's nervous about meeting his new boss. She's a woman." Eva smiled.

She was so pretty when she smiled. For a moment, he forgot why he couldn't share his orchard with her. "Girl bosses are the worse."

"How many women have you worked for?"

He chuckled at her raised hackles. "Just you."

"But I work for you, remember?"

"Everyone knows you're the one telling me what to do."

She leaned against the railing. "Ah, but for how long?"

How long indeed. But he needed to give her some

assurance even if he had a hard time feeling it himself. "For as long as you want it."

Her brown eyes widened. "That's good to know."

The space between them seemed to shrink. He wouldn't mind taking her out now, tonight. Forget the meeting.

"Thanks, Peece."

He nodded. "I'll see you Sunday morning then." He skipped down a couple steps and then turned around. "Eva?"

"Yeah?" She hadn't moved.

"Don't wear a dress Sunday."

She folded her arms and grinned. "Not something I do."

"Too bad." He gave her a wink and took the rest of the stairs.

Eva heard the revving of a motorcycle in the driveway and called out to Beth. "I gotta go. See you at church."

Grabbing her windbreaker, she dashed out the door.

Adam stood beside a big black Harley wearing a black leather jacket and jeans. He was the perfect image of a bad boy. Eva wasn't immune to that kind of picture. She wasn't immune to Adam.

He took off his helmet and smiled. "Hey."

"Hey, yourself." She cautiously eyed his bike. It

looked far more stable than her brother's old motorcycle. Sinclair used to scare the wits out of her by going way too fast.

Adam reached into one of the side bags that hung near the rear wheels. He produced another small, Harley-style helmet. "For you, but it might mess up your hair."

"Like I care." She handed him a vinyl portfolio. "Do you have room for this?"

"What is it?"

"My business outline."

His eyes narrowed, but he placed it safely into the compartment. "Are you going to be okay? Do you want a test drive?"

Eva shook her head as she strapped on the helmet. "I'll be fine. I see that the passenger seat has handles."

He laughed. "That's it?"

"I've ridden motorcycles before. Sinclair had one. It's still in the garage."

He gave her an odd look. "I'll never understand women."

"Why?"

"All that fuss about you not being fond of motorcycles?"

Eva shrugged. Her hesitation had more to do with where she'd hang on than anything else. Adam's bike had sturdy-looking handles under the passenger seat that came with a short backrest. She wouldn't have to hold on to Adam.

Unless she wanted to. She tossed that tempting thought aside. "Don't go too fast."

"I'll go as fast or slow as you want." He swung onto his seat and started the engine. She heard the throaty growl and realized it wasn't that loud. Not like some of the bikes she'd heard thundering through town. Adam revved it more than necessary for show. "Climb on."

Eva grasped his shoulder as she slipped up onto the seat behind him, and away they went.

It was early for church, so they took a detour north along the shore of Lake Michigan. The air felt crisp and the sun peeked out from behind cottonball clouds. True to his word, Adam didn't speed. The deep rumble of his motorcycle lulled her as he drove at a leisurely pace. He seemed to take in the beauty of the lake and hills as much as she did. He even slowed down to stare at a field of grazing sheep.

When they pulled into the church parking lot, it was already filled with cars. Way more than normal.

"Wow, it's packed," she said.

"It's Mother's Day. Must be a lot of visitors here." Adam slipped off his helmet and hung it from the handlebars.

Eva pleaded silently, *Please not today, Lord.* Would Todd and his wife attend? Frozen chains of dread slowed her steps, as if she'd been harnessed to a plow.

Before walking into the sanctuary, Eva scanned the pews until she spotted a pair of broad shoulders that stood above the others. The hair on the back of her neck bristled when the guy turned around as if sensing her. Todd stared straight at her.

Her stomach turned and she backed up, right into Adam.

His hands gently squeezed her upper arms. "What is it?"

"Can we leave?"

"That guy's here, isn't he?"

She nodded.

"Come on." He took her by the hand and led her down the steps into the parking lot.

Feeling dizzy, she braced herself against his motorcycle, trying to catch her breath.

She felt Adam watching her. He stood near enough if needed but he didn't crowd her. What he must be thinking, she couldn't imagine. His silence helped rather than hindered, but the space he gave her wasn't what she wanted. Not this time. She'd never felt so alone. And cold. She looked up.

His blue eyes were filled with concern. "You okay?"

She shook her head, fighting tears and stepped toward him. Without asking permission, she unzipped his leather jacket and curled into him. The warmth of his body seeped through her, calming the icy tremors that threatened to shake her apart.

After a few seconds, she felt his arms come around her. He stroked her back and kissed her hair, her temple. He tipped her chin up and brushed his lips lightly across hers. It was nice. Comforting.

"Maybe we better forget the picnic," he said softly.

She nodded.

"You want to talk about this?" His voice was barely above a whisper, his arms still safe and protective around her.

Eva breathed deep, battling the desire to tell him everything. She wanted to. Her heart ached with it. She had to. "While we were dating..."

Eva took another deep breath.

Adam pulled her a little closer.

"While we were dating, Todd attacked me." There, she'd finally said it. Finally admitted what had happened. Her knees wobbled but she remained standing, even if plastered against Adam for support.

Adam drew back and searched her face. "Did he—" His eyes widened in alarm. "How'd he hurt you?"

The anger she read in Adam's eyes made her think twice about the details. She could tell he thought the worst. The last thing she needed was Adam marching into service and dragging Todd out by the collar. "No, no. He tried to force me. And he would have, but I—" She looked at the cleft in Adam's chin. "I got away."

"Have you talked to anyone about this?"

He meant a professional. A counselor. She shook her head. "Can we still ride?"

Adam rubbed her shoulders and then he grabbed her helmet, hanging next to his own. Gently, he positioned it on her head without looking at her. "Chin up."

She obeyed, staring at his grim face while he secured the strap of her helmet.

He brushed his knuckles against her cheek, his gaze focused on her face but not her eyes. He didn't look her in the eyes. He climbed on and started the engine. "Get on, Eva."

Again, she did what he told her.

With a spit of gravel, Adam tore out onto the road. He slowed when they got to town. Driving through LeNaro took only minutes, and then they were on back roads heading west. She didn't care where they went or for how long. She didn't even care that Adam was driving much faster than he'd promised this morning.

Only one thought ran through her brain and brought tears to her eyes all over again.

He thinks I'm damaged goods.

Chapter Ten

Adam blindly drove. He'd never felt more ill equipped to help someone. He had no idea who to deal with whatever Eva had experienced. How could a guy twice her size physically hurt her? Her prickly mistrust made a whole lot of sense now. An abusive relationship could do that. His Eva had been abused. He gritted his teeth, vowing to never let that brute anywhere near Eva again. He revved the engine and sped forward.

Somewhere along the road, he felt Eva wrap her arms around his waist to hang on. His heart tumbled. He reached down and patted Eva's leg, hoping to convey that he'd be there for her. That he cared. That he wouldn't push her. Wouldn't rush things between them.

Dear Lord, be with her. And help me not be a jerk.

He continued to pray like he always did when

riding his Harley. Something about being on the bike reminded him of God's awesome power and redemptive love. Eva needed to come back to the knowledge that all things were possible in Christ. His impression that she'd distanced herself from God suddenly made sense, too. If she'd open her heart and realize she didn't have to go it alone, she might heal.

Could he show her the way back?

He slipped his hand over Eva's and squeezed.

Eva laid her head against Adam's back, thankful for his touch of encouragement. She stared at the grassy stretches of open fields and homes dotting the landscape as Adam traveled south. They buzzed through a couple small towns along route 616 until they hit the aquamarine waters of Glen Lake. Then they turned north toward the Sleeping Bear Dunes National Park.

Adam might be right about her needing professional help. Holding on to the hurt wasn't getting her anywhere but running away from church service whenever Todd showed up. It was her church and she'd gone there since she was a child. How could she allow that lowlife to steal away her comfort there, her security?

She tipped her head toward the sky. The gentle sway of the bike rocked her like a baby seeking comfort from cutting teeth. It hurt. *Lord, how it hurt to see Todd.*

Show me how to get over this, God. Please? Can you even hear me anymore? Do you want to?

Eva stared at Adam's black leather-clad back. The newly trimmed edge of his dark hair just barely flipped up from under his helmet. She ran her finger against the crisp texture of that edge. Thick, his hair felt thick. Strong. She'd never expected Adam Peece would be someone she'd turn to for strength. Who knew?

She felt Adam slow the bike and then he turned into an ice-cream stand's parking lot. He stopped and flipped down the kickstand, then stood, balancing the motorcycle for her. "I thought we could use a break."

"Perfect timing because I'm thirsty." Eva slid off his motorcycle and got in line.

When Adam stepped next to her, she gave him a gentle poke of her elbow. "Thanks for the ride. It really helped."

He nodded. "No problem. Maybe we should find another church?"

His offer to go with her warmed her heart. It wasn't as if they were a couple, but his support flew like a schoolyard flag announcing that he truly cared. "Thanks, but I'll figure this out."

"You don't have to do it alone, you know."

She nodded. Whether he referred to getting help or accepting his didn't matter. She appreciated the offer. "Don't say anything to Ryan, okay?"

"I won't." He gave her shoulder a gentle squeeze.

When it was their turn, Eva ordered a cone dipped in chocolate and an ice water. Adam settled on a banana split after draining one of the two bottled waters he'd fished out of an ice-filled cooler. When the clerk gave her a total, Eva pulled out her wallet from the front pouch of her windbreaker.

"I've got this." Adam offered up a ten.

She blocked his path to the window. "You drove. I'm paying."

He chuckled and let her have her way.

Once settled at a picnic table under a weeping willow tree, Eva bit into her ice cream, sending bits of the hard chocolate shell tumbling down the front of her peach-colored jacket. A river of melting soft-serve ice cream followed with a drip that landed near a smear of chocolate. Great! She licked her cone furiously.

"Here." Adam handed her a few napkins with a grin. "Can't you eat ice cream without making a mess?"

"Guess not." She should be embarrassed, but she wasn't. It amazed her how comfortable she felt around Adam. And now he knew what she'd been hiding for two years. It felt good that he knew. Physically safe and secure even though her heart inched that much closer to danger.

"Tell me about your business plan."

Wiping her mouth, she smiled and plunged ahead.

Relieved to talk about something other than what had happened to her. "Obviously you'd remain the controlling partner since I couldn't afford much of a buy-in."

He winked at her. "Obviously."

Eva's hopes soared. "As you know, my father grew predominately tart cherries, but I think a move toward sweet cherries with an eye on turning Marsh Orchards into a retail farm is the better bet for self-sufficiency. The B and B would only enhance what the orchard provided."

She waited to gauge how receptive he was, but his expression didn't give anything away.

"Keep talking," he said.

Eva lifted her eyebrows. "You've never said if you're going to change the name."

"I haven't thought about it."

"What about Peecetorini Farm?"

His brow furrowed. "Where'd you hear that?"

"Your sister told me it's your family's real name. I think it's a beautiful name. So lush and full."

"My sister's got a big mouth." Adam dug out the cherry from his sundae and popped it in his mouth.

"Don't you like it?"

"'Course I do. It's my ancestry."

"But?"

Adam shrugged.

"Is it the legal paperwork involved in going back to it?"

"Not at all."

He set down his empty sundae dish and then stuffed a couple of wadded-up napkins in it when the breeze skittered the plastic bowl across the picnic table. "I've walked away from the family business a couple times. Changing my name back to Peecetorini sends the final message, don't you think? The final adios that this time, I'm really done."

"You're telling me that as Adam Peecetorini, you couldn't go back to Peece Canning?"

"It's a symbolic thing."

Peece Canning Corporation was Adam's safety net if cherry farming didn't work out for him. Leonard Peece might have set the net, but Adam wasn't ready to cut all ties. All the more reason for Eva to have some sort of ownership, keeping some of the land tied to her.

"It's something to consider. New name for a new owner and new direction." Eva bit into the crunchy part of her cone.

"Down the road, maybe. For now, I like Marsh Orchards just fine."

Eva went on to describe a timeline for moving toward a U-pick cherry farm and market that would bring consumers to them. Ultimately they'd have more control over profits versus relying solely on commercial processors.

"Well." Eva finally took a breath. "What do you think?"

"I think I'd like a look at your outline."

"I made an extra copy for you." She moved to retrieve it, but he stopped her with a touch of his hand.

"You can give it to me when I drop you off. Look, Eva, I'm sticking with my original decision. I want input. I want to hear what you have in mind. You've got some great ideas, but don't get too excited, okay?"

"I understand." But she wasn't giving up.

He smiled then. "So, you like the Peecetorini name?"

"I do."

The following week Adam and Eva applied a bee-friendly fungicide to the tart cherries. They'd moved quickly, using the truck mount sprayer attached to Eva's pickup. The only delay was a touch-and-go weather report forecasting two days' worth of rain that turned out to be nothing more than an afternoon cloudburst.

He could tell that Eva's zeal for a partnership hadn't waned. Even though she hadn't said a word about whether he'd looked at her outline, he knew that question lurked in her brain. He'd catch her deep in thought and knew better than to ask what she was thinking.

Adam was impressed with her concise business plan. Her ideas for increasing profit looked sound and the timeline she referenced to put them into action made sense. She'd make a good business owner, but that didn't mean he'd revisit her offer. His answer had to be no until this season was over. Until he knew there'd be a next season for him.

After lunch, Adam drained his bottled water and stretched. "So, tonight we move the bees back out?"

"Aunt Jamee is bringing over dinner. Ryan said he'd be over to help load the hives so it should go pretty quick."

"Good. I'm beat."

Eva shook her head.

"I know, I know. Wait till harvest." But Adam would have hired help by then. Hopefully one of them would be Eva's father.

He had already gone over with Bob Marsh his list of summertime workers found in the barn's filing cabinets. Eva might not know the past couple of seasons' workers since she'd been at pastry school. So, he ran the names by Bob to be sure. Adam didn't care to bring back trouble.

By the time they headed for the house, Adam spied the flatbed belonging to Eva's aunt and uncle parked in the driveway. Once in the kitchen, Adam inhaled the rich aroma of pot roast and his stomach answered with a deprived rumble.

"Dinner's ready. I'll have it on the table in a few minutes." Jamee wore an outlandish apron depicting bees dressed in army camouflage. Embroidered along the front read *Bee All You Can Bee Farm*.

"Nice apron." Adam sidled up to the sink and grabbed the liquid soap.

Jamee snapped him with a towel. "Take it to the bathroom, Adam. I have vegetables to drain."

"Oww." He caught Eva's look of amusement.

"She won't let anyone wash up while she's in the kitchen. I'll use the one upstairs, and you can have the powder room." Eva made to leave.

"It's not sanitary to wash off your dirt near my food." Jamee turned to him with a nod toward where Eva had just exited. "And she has a bad habit of leaving the mayonnaise out. I found it on the counter today."

"I heard that," Eva yelled from the hall.

"Her ice cream eating is pretty bad, too. I'll have to keep my eye on her," Adam said.

"You do that." Her aunt winked at him.

Adam could imagine Eva rolling her eyes at that comment. Obviously her aunt had matchmaking on her mind. She was as bad as Beth. He had money and the family farm and Eva wanted in on the orchard. Made sense that Eva's family would hint around them hooking up.

He wanted to, but the timing had to be right. Things seemed to be getting more complicated with a partnership offer, Eva's past relationship and his death knell by harvest lurking on the horizon. Adam needed to keep things simple. The next date he'd planned was the research center's fundraiser. It'd be work and fun rolled together. And a safe place. He didn't want Eva to feel pressured.

When he returned from washing up, Ryan and Larry entered the kitchen while Beth finished setting the table. Adam slid into a chair facing the activity. "Does it matter where I sit?"

"Nope." Beth placed a bowl of salad onto the table.

Larry sat next to him. "Perfect evening to move the hives. It's cooling down nicely and the bees are settling back into their homes. We should be able to get to work soon after dinner."

Adam nodded. "It's supposed to get cold tonight, around thirty-five to forty."

"Let's hope that's as cool as it gets." Jamee set a basket covered with a towel on the table.

That was what Adam prayed. Northern Michigan wasn't out of the woods when it came to frost. He lifted the cloth to spy steaming hot rolls. What was taking so long to get everyone seated?

Eva entered the kitchen and her aunt handed her a covered dish. She set it down and took the seat across from him.

"Don't even think of lifting that lid, Adam. The veggies will get cold."

"Leave him alone, Jamee. He's hungry." Larry came to his defense. "She's one of the caterers for the research center fundraiser this year."

Adam smiled at the beekeeper's wife. "Then I look forward to it even more."

"You're going?" Beth took her seat.

Adam nodded.

Jamee finally came to the table. "It's quite the black-tie affair."

"Please, don't remind me," Ryan groaned.

Jamee stood behind her chair. "Eva, I wonder, do you think you could help out serving?"

"I was hoping Eva might agree to go with me." Adam spoke up before Eva had the chance to answer her aunt.

A hush fell over the table, but Adam kept his focus on Eva. Would she go with him? He'd bought the tickets at the meeting he'd attended with Ryan more than a week ago. He'd had every intention of asking Eva to go, but he'd hesitated. Worried that she might say no.

Eva looked up from fiddling with her napkin. "When is it?"

"This weekend," Adam said.

Jamee smiled. "Go have fun, Eva. I won't need you after all. The college kids are home."

"These things are never fun," Ryan added.

"That depends," Adam said.

"On what?" Beth asked with a grin.

Adam looked straight at Eva. "My date."

That brought down the house with good-natured teasing and whistles. But Eva looked wary and she hadn't yet agreed to go.

"Good morning," Eva found Adam with Ryan in the kitchen making coffee. Again, Adam had stayed at Ryan's after moving the beehives. The hives were heavy after ten days in the orchard and that boded well for honey.

"What's on our list of chores today?" Adam leaned against the island with cup in hand while the coffeemaker chugged and hissed.

"After you and Ryan set the fly traps, we can spray fungicide on the sweet cherries."

"How do those traps work?"

Ryan intervened. "The insect counts help determine if an insecticide is needed. That way you're not spraying needlessly."

Eva grabbed eggs and bacon from the fridge. "My father did things the way his father had shown him. But Ryan convinced him to try some new things."

"And what do you think?" Adam poured his coffee and then offered the pot to her brother.

"My father showed me what to look for. You

have to know what's going on in your own orchard. Ryan's a good researcher, but he gets crazy with monitoring and reporting. My father didn't care if his farm was certified as environmentally friendly or not. He did what he thought best for a quality crop."

"At Peece Canning, the organic green beans fetched a higher price."

"You can't farm cherries completely organic. There are too many pests to deal with. And the weather plays a huge part. Too much humidity and fungus becomes a bigger problem," Eva said.

"She's right," her brother backed her up.

Eva smiled. "It's up to you to decide which market you're going to tap. Retail or commercial."

Adam nodded. "Something to think about."

Despite catching on to the work and his affinity with engines, Adam Peece was no grower. Not yet anyway. He needed her to help make it happen and that was what she counted on.

After breakfast they rode out on four-wheelers to set up the flytraps. The ground was littered with fallen blossoms, and the breeze swirled the remaining petals, making the orchard look like a shaken snowglobe. The sun filtered in between the leafy-green trees and there was no place Eva would rather be.

Driving at a sedate pace with the supplies in her

wagon, Eva watched Ryan and Adam race along the edge of the orchard. She couldn't help but yell, "What are you, twelve?"

"Sometimes!" Adam hollered back.

She laughed. She hadn't agreed to go with Adam to that fundraiser. Beth told her she had to prove that she could handle being his partner. Schmoozing was part of that, even though it'd be a daunting task considering the lack of glitz in her closet. Eva hadn't worn a formal dress since her high-school prom.

When she caught up with the guys, they set up the traps along the edge of the woods bordering the orchard.

Ryan made notations while Adam and Eva took a water break in the shade.

"Have you decided about going with me to the fundraiser?" Adam asked.

Eva looked down at her booted feet and kicked a clump of grass. He had asked her as if it was a date, which meant it wasn't only business. "It'd be good for me to go."

He stepped closer. "I'd like you to."

"I'm no good at mingling."

Adam gently grabbed her hand and brought it to his lips for the briefest kiss. "Then stick close to me. I'll do the talking."

She smiled, even though her insides were fluttering like blossom petals in the wind. "Promise?"

"I'll pick you up at seven, Saturday night."

Eva glanced at her brother. He was busy charting the traps. There was no way she'd refuse. "I'll be ready."

Chapter Eleven

Saturday morning, Beth made herself comfy on Eva's bed and scrunched up her nose with disapproval. "You can't wear that to the fundraiser."

"No?" Eva held the newly purchased pantsuit against her body and surveyed her image in the mirror. It wasn't so bad. She'd tried it on yesterday at the boutique in town after stopping at the bank. She'd been pleased by how comfortable and light it felt. It had even been on sale.

She slipped into a pair of black pumps and ignored the orange cuffs of her pajamas peeking below the belled bottoms of the pantsuit. Her reflection showed a whole lot of black material. "Why not? Black's supposed to be elegant."

Beth clicked her tongue with schoolteacher ease. "Little black dresses, yes. Black pantsuits? Not so much. You look like you're going to an office party or a funeral."

Panic slithered up Eva's spine. "Adam's picking me up at seven. What am I supposed to do now?"

Beth grinned. "I thought you'd never ask."

Eva cringed at the overly excited gleam in her roommate's eye. Shopping with Beth usually meant large sums of money were about to be lost. Eva recognized the glazed look, but she did need help. "What do you have in mind?"

"First, let's have breakfast." Her roommate pointed at the offending outfit. "We can return *that* on our way to Traverse City."

"But—"

"But what?"

Eva shrugged. She had any number of things to do today, but she'd feel more confident getting ready for tonight's fundraiser with Beth's help. She should have known better than to attempt formal fashion without her. Draping her arm around her friend, Eva gave her a quick squeeze. "Thanks, Beth. Once again you're saving my skin."

"It's what I do. Now, let's get moving. We've got a full day ahead."

After several hours and too many stores to count, Eva's head pounded, but she wouldn't give up. Each dress selected was quickly discarded in the dressing room. Too tight, too skimpy, too costly. And then Eva tried on a ruby-colored halter dress made with filmy fabric. She looked in the mirror and smiled.

Stepping out of the fitting room, she held her breath and waited for her roommate's opinion.

Beth's eyes lit up. "That's it. That's the one."

Eva let out her breath with a whoosh and twirled. The translucent material floated and then settled into generous folds of shimmering silk organza just above her knee. She didn't need a fairy godmother for this ball, not when she had her best friend. And then Eva checked the price tag and her spirits plummeted. "I can't."

Beth frowned. "Don't look at that, Eva."

"It's too much."

"Think of it as an investment. You're investing in your future partnership with Adam." Beth winked.

Eva chewed her bottom lip. She'd paid down her credit card balance for her loan application. She'd received the approval but hadn't closed yet. Would the bank know if she racked up her balance again? Would they care?

"Buy it, Eva. It's perfect on you. We have to look at shoes, too. You can't wear those black pumps. My mother has an antique evening bag that will match. And you'll need your hair done."

Eva tuned out Beth's verbal To Do list and quickly did the math. It wasn't good. The dress cost a small fortune. Staring at her reflection in the mirror, Eva squared her shoulders. Spend money to make money, right?

Who was she trying to fool? There was only one reason she'd buy this dress and shoes and visit the salon. She'd face her finances tomorrow—because tonight all she cared about was impressing Adam. And it had nothing to do with business.

Adam smoothed the front of his tuxedo jacket before knocking on Eva's door. He'd fussed over his appearance as if he'd never been to a black-tie affair before.

Beth answered it with a whistle. "My, my, don't you look pretty."

He laughed as he stepped into the kitchen. Beth's comment sounded like something Eva might say. "Men don't want to be pretty, but thanks."

"Eva will be down in a minute."

He nodded and ran his finger around the inside of his collar. He'd made the bow tie too tight. He'd even pulled out the family's antique Corvette from the town house garage. This afternoon he'd washed and waxed it in hopes of wowing Eva.

"Want something to drink? Lemonade or a pop?" Beth offered.

"I'm fine." But he wasn't.

He'd escorted any number of women to events like this without a passing thought. Tonight, he felt like a nervous teen picking up the girl he'd finally asked to prom. Only this was no girl. This was Eva. The woman he'd spent hours with in the orchard talking up a storm or quietly working side by side. A woman he admired and had grown to care deeply about.

He kicked at the braided rug under the kitchen table with the shiny black toe of his shoe. "So, what are you doing tonight?"

Beth shrugged. "I have papers to grade."

Adam couldn't believe a girl like Beth didn't have a date. "Quiet way to pass a Saturday night."

"I like quiet." Beth's attention shifted toward the hall.

"Sorry to keep you waiting." Eva stood in the kitchen. Her hair had been swept up, revealing an expanse of neck above bare shoulders that shimmered in the light.

Adam forgot to breathe. He blinked a couple times and then swallowed hard.

"Ready?" Her cheeks were rosy.

"Yeah." But Adam continued to stare. The dress she wore floated when she moved, like a blossom petal in the breeze. Soft and feminine. "Eva, you look… You're—"

"Nice, huh?" Beth added.

"Really nice." Adam made for the door and opened it. It'd been a long time since he'd been struck speechless.

Eva passed by him with an enticing wave of her floral perfume as she scooped up a wrap draped across a chair. "See you later tonight, Beth."

"I won't wait up," her roommate said.

Eva's cheeks blushed even darker.

And Adam tugged at his collar. He kept scanning Eva from the big silver hoop earrings she wore down to her strappy high-heeled sandals that were also silver. Her toenails were painted the same rich ruby color as her dress. An electric current of anticipation hummed through him.

He offered Eva his hand as they walked from the porch to the driveway.

"Whoa! Nice car," Eva said.

"I thought this was more suited for black tie than the Jeep."

"We could have taken my truck and caused a stir. I think my muffler's going." Eva gave him an impish grin.

"I can replace it for you." Adam opened the passenger-side door for her.

She slipped into the seat and then looked up with an amused glint in her eyes. "Where'd you learn to do that?"

With the seat belt in hand, he leaned down and buckled her in. His face inches from hers he said, "You can learn a lot from magazines."

"Good to know." Her voice dipped to barely a whisper.

Adam looked back into her eyes. Then, with a smile, he straightened, walked around to his side and slid in behind the wheel.

"I took auto mechanics in high school, much to my father's annoyance. Like I said before, I tinker." Turning the key, he gave a satisfied nod at the gravel-laced purr of the Corvette's engine.

Eva laughed, sounding completely at ease. "You are such a motor head."

Even though she teased him, Adam caught the respect shining in her eyes. He sat straighter. "You know it."

It didn't take long before they arrived at the high-end resort where the fundraiser was held. After he'd pulled the car up to the front, Adam went around to the passenger side and opened the door for Eva.

"Thank you." Again she gave him her hand.

Her fingernails had been painted, too. Not a trace of the cute farm girl remained. This exquisite woman made Adam nervous. How was he supposed to keep his wits around her?

He tossed his keys to the valet and escorted Eva into the building. "Have you been here before?"

"I worked a wedding here once that Aunt Jamee had catered. What about you?" She turned her face toward his and he noticed that her eyes had been outlined in smoky colors. Her lips were slicked with deep cherry-red gloss.

"No. Never." His hand found the small of her back and he steered her toward the ballroom. He scanned the area for Ryan and gave him a nod when he found him. Better to get the mingling out of the way so he could monopolize his farm manager's attention the rest of the evening.

Eva's brother made his way toward them. "Whoa, Eva, look at you."

Adam saw the color rise to her cheeks again. His hand remained comfortably against her back.

"You're pretty dashing yourself, Ryan. Where'd you get the tux?"

Ryan looked around the room. "Rented it."

"Is your new boss here? Point her out." Eva gave her brother a playful smile.

"I haven't seen her yet, but it's still early. Adam, there's a new grower I'd like you to meet if I can pry you away from my sister."

"She comes with us. Lead the way." He made to follow, but Eva stayed put. He wondered if Ryan's comment had offended her. Letting his hand drop, he turned to her. "Anything wrong?"

"No. You go ahead. I'm going to say hello to my aunt. She's around here somewhere and she'll be disappointed if I don't show her my dress. I don't wear too many."

He wouldn't mind seeing her wear more. He gave her a wink. "I'll find you."

Eva watched Adam walk away. He wore his tuxedo well. Sleek, perfect, expensive. No tuxedo rental for Adam Peece. He probably had a closet full of them. He'd even slicked his hair back. Funny, but she didn't know a single farmer who put gel in his hair.

She made her way to the kitchens and slipped between the swinging double doors. Her aunt piled a tray with hors d'oeuvres. "How's it going?"

"Oh, Eva, you shouldn't be back here, you'll get dirty." Her aunt stood back and scanned her from head to toe. "You're stunning."

With her hair done up in a swirl at the back of her head, Eva felt like an out-of-place princess. She'd sought out her aunt's encouragement. She knew she'd wowed Adam when he picked her up, but here at the party there were many gowns more impressive than hers worn by more beautiful women. Not that Adam seemed to notice, but could she really hope to hold her own in his world? She didn't have her mother nearby to run to for boosting her courage, so Aunt Jamee was the next best thing.

"Beth helped me find the dress. So, who else is catering?" Eva popped a stuffed mushroom in her mouth.

Her aunt drew her close and her black chef's hat flopped forward. "Who else?"

"Charlotte?" There was only one other caterer in LeNaro, her aunt Jamee's competition and their second cousin. The one no one liked.

"She bribed Miss Winnie out of retirement for tonight."

Eva expressed the expected shock. "I thought Miss Winnie cooked for a treatment center."

Her aunt looked indignant but nodded. "If I'd have known Miss Winnie would do a weekend stint, I'd have called her myself. I cut my catering eye-teeth with her, you know."

She knew. But when her aunt gave orders for the baked Brie to be served, Eva turned to leave. "I better let you do your thing."

Her aunt squeezed her hand. "Thank you, beauty. Dance your toes off tonight."

"I'll try." Eva didn't expect too many dance partners. Unless Adam asked her. That thought sent a shiver up her spine. She'd be surprised if Adam didn't dance as well as he looked. Eva hoped to find out.

With a deep breath, Eva left the kitchens with every intention of returning to the party. She wasn't proving herself capable of mixing in Adam's circles by hiding out. The worst part about events like this was spewing inane chatter, hoping someone might find it interesting. Squaring her shoulders, she made a beeline for the balcony off the ballroom. Hiding out had its advantages, too.

The air was warm and smelled of cut grass and newly turned soil ready for planting spring flowers. She breathed deep.

"What are you doing out here?"

Eva turned at the sound of Adam's voice. "Catching some fresh air."

"Before you suffocate from the stuffiness?" He stood next to her. "Some of these people are scraping the ceiling with their noses."

She laughed.

He propped his elbows on the marble railing and gazed out at Lake Leelanau. "Gorgeous night."

The western sky glowed pink from the sun that had set. She pointed through the trees that made skinny black silhouettes against the twilight sky. "There's the moon. Not even a half."

"Yeah."

Eva remained quiet, watching the way the moon cast a sliver of shimmering light across the black water of the lake. She felt the tension in Adam, the way his back remained stiff as he gazed at that slice of moon. Maybe he didn't like these kinds of events either.

She cleared her throat. "I received good news on my loan application. I'm approved for more than I expected."

He faced her. The cleft in the middle of his stern chin looked deeper in the dark. His blue eyes black. "My answer's still no, Eva."

"You haven't even heard my offer." She hated the whine that crept into her voice.

"I don't need to."

"I'd be good for you—" Her heart skipped. "For your business, I mean. For the orchard."

He stepped closer and her heart leaped.

His lips curved into a soft smile. "You're already good for me. Can we talk about this later? I'd like to introduce you to a few folks and then grab some food before dinner's served."

She'd rather stay out here and hash out a partnership deal. "Wait, you want to eat before we eat?"

"Come on." He held out his hand.

Without hesitation, she took it.

He threaded his fingers through hers. "I know these kind of events are a pain, but there's a real benefit to putting our faces before the processors. I want these people to know Marsh Orchards is alive and well. If you're with me, it'll reinforce that."

Eva nodded. Put like that, how could she refuse to schmooze? But then, to keep her hand wrapped in his, she'd follow him anywhere. "As long as you stay with me. I'm no good on my own."

"You got it." He led her back to the ballroom where the band played soft music.

The songs were barely detectable over the din of conversation, but Eva could hear it well enough as Adam navigated them easily through the crowd. He introduced her to a few growers that were part of a co-op. Then they moved on to meet a national fruit processor whose eyebrows shot up toward his fake hairline when Adam explained that Eva was his farm manager, not his wife.

But Eva's stomach had flipped when she heard the lilt in Adam's deep voice. The sound of him pronouncing the word *wife* rang through her brain over and over. Beth was right. Eva wanted to be Adam's reason to stay. And she couldn't help but wonder what it might be like if they ran the orchard together as husband and wife. Life partners instead of business partners.

Adam sighed with relief when the dinner announcement was finally made. Clarifying his relationship with Eva was getting old quick. Even people Eva knew asked if he was her boyfriend. He'd almost said yes to see how Eva might react. Was she ready for that step?

Bigger question—was he?

There was only one way to find out.

Once seated and served their appetizers, Adam concentrated on the program delivered by Ryan's research team regarding the challenges facing today's fruit grower. He glanced at Eva. She swirled her appetizers around her plate with a fork.

"Not hungry?" he whispered.

She leaned close and whispered back, "I don't like stuffed grape leaves."

He moved his plate toward hers. "Hand 'em over."

She rolled the appetizers from her plate to his

with her knife. She stifled a giggle when her knife screeched against the china, drawing annoyed stares from their tablemates.

"Nice move," he whispered.

She gave him a mischief-filled grin that made him wish they were back out on that balcony.

By the time dinner was over and dessert and coffee had been served, all Adam could think about was getting Eva away from everyone. He wondered if this might have been how the first Adam felt when Eve offered up the apple. Only his Eva offered a business deal he couldn't make and a future he couldn't plan until he broke even after harvest.

He'd love to cement a more permanent working relationship with Eva, but he cared too much for it to be only business. If he made mistakes, he wanted it on his dime, not hers. That farmhouse was all she had left of her family's legacy. He wouldn't let her risk losing it.

If the balcony was better left off-limits, at least he could take her out onto the floor. "Wanna dance?"

She looked at him with wide eyes and hesitated only a moment before giving him her hand. "Absolutely."

The band played a big-band version of Van Morrison's "Brown-Eyed Girl." Perfect. He led Eva toward a far corner of the dance floor that was already filling up.

"I haven't done this in a while, so forgive me if I step all over you," Eva said.

"No problem. I'm used to you hurting me." He twirled her away from him and then tugged her back, winding his arm loosely around her waist. She felt so good in his arms.

She laughed. "Hey, how can you say that?"

"Hmm, you froze my fingers, knocked me over, poisoned me and got me stung by your uncle's bees."

"You got yourself stung. If you'd have left them alone…"

"I know, I know. They would have flown away." He spun her again.

They stayed on the dance floor through a couple more songs and Adam could not have cared less about mingling. Eva's steps were uncertain at first, but after another upbeat tune, she snuggled when he pulled her closer.

That balcony beckoned.

"Want to get some air?" he asked.

"Sure." Did he detect a catch in her voice?

He took her hand to leave, but the lights dimmed and the band began a slow, slow song. He couldn't resist the excuse to pull Eva even closer. "We can't go yet."

She looked up at him with those smoky-rimmed eyes. "I guess not."

As they swayed to the music, he didn't look away

from her. As he stared into those big, chocolate-brown eyes of hers, their steps faltered until finally they made slow circles in the same spot.

He ran his finger along the side of her cheek. "You're beautiful."

Pleasant surprise registered on her face. "Really?"

He tightened his hold. "Really."

She smiled and dipped her head onto his shoulder.

Breathing in the scent of her hair, Adam brushed his lips across her forehead.

She pulled back and gazed at him with a question in her eyes.

He recognized it as the same one he had asked himself often enough. Was there any point to ignoring this connection between them any longer?

Forgetting that they were on a crowded dance floor, Adam slipped her arms up around his neck. Feeling her fingers tease the back of his hair, he lowered his head.

They fit perfectly together. Maybe she really had been made for him. Just for him.

Inhaling Eva's sigh, Adam kissed her.

Chapter Twelve

Eva waited for Adam to put his ridiculously fast car into Park before she said anything. When he turned off the engine, she turned in the passenger seat. "Thank you for a lovely evening."

He faced her. "Look, Eva, about tonight—"

She placed her finger on his lips. Eva didn't want to discuss what happened on the dance floor. It was magical and special. She didn't want to ruin it by breaking it down. "I had fun."

"Me, too." He grabbed her hand and slowly kissed her palm.

With a start, Eva pulled her hand away. She took a calming breath, but it did nothing to ease the nervous shiver than tickled her spine. "Maybe, we should say goodnight."

"You're probably right."

But neither of them made a move to leave.

"Eva." Adam ran his hand through his hair,

messing it up. "I want to explore what we've got going here, but I don't want to rush you into anything you're not ready for."

He was giving her space. After that incredible kiss on the dance floor, Eva was scared to go too fast too soon. "I appreciate that."

Only half of Adam's face was visible from the porch light shining through the windshield, but his smile was sweet. "Then I'll see you tomorrow."

He made her feel like the peanut butter to his jam, but would Adam Peece be satisfied as a PB and J kind of guy when he came from a world of caviar? She'd have to find out. "Good night, Adam."

He flashed her another smile. "That's the second time you've used my name. The first was in the emergency room."

Eva shuddered when she remembered Adam's mottled face from the allergic reaction. "I still feel bad about that."

He shrugged it off. "I like the way my name sounds coming from you."

She liked saying it. Even more, she liked pairing it with her own name. Adam and Eva. Did it get any cornier than that? "I can't promise you that I'll use it all the time."

He chuckled. "Don't worry. I'd miss you calling me Peece."

She slipped out of the passenger side, before she

gave in and leaned close. "Well, then, good night, Peece."

"Eva, wait." He got out and came around the front of the car. "Let me at least walk you to the door."

She gave him a half-grin. "I suppose I owe you another kiss after such a wonderful night, huh?"

When they got to the porch step, Adam's hand slid down her arm, halting her. "You don't owe me anything, Eva. I'll never push you that way. Got it?"

She looked into his serious eyes. He'd taken her off-the-cuff comment as an insult. Staring at him, she battled between her desire to make it up to him and the common sense to accept his patience. "I'm sorry."

He gently squeezed her hand. "Good night, Eva."

Adam watched her slip quietly into the house before he trotted down the porch steps and got back into the car. After she switched off the outside light, he backed out of her driveway.

Humming the song they'd slow-danced to, Adam drove home. He'd never been in a long-term relationship, and Eva was the kind of girl who wouldn't settle for anything less. He'd keep his promise not to rush.

God?

He didn't even know how to pray for the two of them.

Give me wisdom. Help me show her that she can trust me. That I won't hurt her—

He stopped mid-prayer. He'd never been serious about a woman before. How was this supposed to go? He certainly didn't have a solid example of marital longevity to follow.

All he knew was that he thought about Eva day and night. For now, that was enough to build on. The kiss they'd shared on the dance floor only made him want more. But Eva wasn't ready for more, and he'd respect that. He shifted into overdrive, pushing the gas pedal harder than he should.

Problem was, Adam wasn't so good at waiting. He didn't want to blow his chances by being impatient. Eva was worth waiting for. No matter how long it took.

At first Eva didn't hear the ring of her phone over the din of the mowing attachment on her tractor. She flipped open her cell and read the caller's name. *Adam.*

It felt like butterflies were trapped in her belly. "Yessir?"

"Do you see those clouds coming in from the west?"

Eva stretched her head around. Dark clouds hovered over the lake, already dropping rain with a grayish blur from sky to water. She'd been too busy daydreaming about yours truly to notice them, not to mention that she was mowing the lower section of the orchard, which had a limited view. "I see them."

"How long do we have until that hits?"

"Not long."

"Better get to the barn." Adam hung up.

"Okay," she chirped at her phone. Could he have given her the chance to say something, anything, like maybe "see you in a few minutes"? Why was he being so curt?

Looking over the acreage left to mow, Eva stifled a growl. They'd been on a roll and would have the mowing done by this weekend, Memorial Day weekend. But now...

The air had a definite chill to it. Cold rain was on its way, making it unpleasant for mowing. By the time she pulled the tractor into the barn, the icy water fell, splashing the ground in a soft, steady rhythm. It was the kind of rain that coaxed a person under a blanket with a book or snuggled close for a nap.

She popped down from the tractor while Adam shrugged into a sweatshirt. She looked out of the still-open barn door as rain dripped inside. "Ready to make a run for it?"

He reached behind her father's file cabinet in the corner. Adam had moved in a few things, turning the small space into a makeshift office. He fluffed open a big black umbrella. "I'll walk you to the house."

"I won't melt."

He laughed and tugged her underneath the umbrella. He smelled like freshly cut grass, rain and motor grease. Heady stuff. "You might."

Her pulse picked up speed. "What's that supposed to mean?"

"Sometimes you remind me of spun sugar."

"Cotton candy?" She stopped walking and squinted up at him, hoping he thought she was pretty like a huge pink puff of the stuff.

"The kind you make over pastry. It's hard but fragile."

Her breath hitched as his gaze sucked her in. "I don't break that easy."

"That's because you're staying up on the shelf."

"No, I'm not."

That wasn't quite true. They'd gone out twice this week—to the movies and then to dinner the other night. Both times she'd pulled back too quickly when Adam had tried to kiss her. She liked the safety and control she had on that shelf. But Adam wanted her to step down. Not all the way, but some.

He shook his head like she was a lost cause. "Come on, let's get to the house."

Together they closed the main door and then darted across the driveway and yard, sloshing water as they went. Adam pulled her close under the umbrella, but she still got wet. Her jeans were soaked by the time they got to the porch. Adam's were, too.

They walked into the kitchen warmed by a chicken dinner baking in the oven. Beth's turn to cook.

"Hey, Adam." Her roommate bustled about. "Are you staying for dinner?"

"Love to." He was already kicking off his muddy boots.

Eva slipped out of hers, too. "I'm going to change. Would you like a pair of sweats, Peece?"

He ran his hands through his hair, smoothing the places that stuck out. "Nope. I'm fine."

When she returned, the rain outside had stopped as quickly as it had come. She found Adam in the living room watching the weather forecast and looking worried. "What's up?"

"They're calling for frost tonight."

Her stomach sank. "But isn't the rain going to stick around a while?"

"Quick-moving front with cold, dry arctic air behind it."

Her landline rang with unnerving volume and Eva ran to grab it. "Hello? Hey, Dad. Yeah, yeah, he's here." She handed the cordless to Adam. "It's my father, for you."

"Hey, Bob. What's up?" Adam didn't sound the least surprised to get a call from her dad.

How many calls had he exchanged with Robert Marsh? Eva talked to her folks every weekend, and not once had her father let on how often he talked to Adam. Why hadn't they filled her in?

After he'd handed the phone back to her, Adam headed for the door. "I'll be back."

"Where are you going?"

"To rent some propane heaters."

"Dad, I'll call you later." Eva didn't wait for her father's agreement. She ran out after Adam. "I'll go with you. We can take my truck. You won't fit those things in your Jeep."

He nodded and climbed into the passenger side of her pickup, his cell phone to his ear. Once he ended the call, he buckled in. "The rental place in Traverse City is holding a dozen or so for me."

"We can't protect the whole orchard with that few."

"I know. Your dad's worried about the low spot. If we can keep that area of the orchard warm enough, he said we might be okay."

"Unless it's a bad frost. There's only so much we can do."

Adam shook his head.

"What?"

"That's exactly what your dad said you'd say."

Eva gritted her teeth. "That it might be a lost cause?"

"That and you'd complain about the expense."

She slammed the stick shift into the next gear, pleased that her truck ran quietly since Adam had worked on it. He had more talent than she'd given him credit for. "It's your money."

"Another reason not to become partners. You give me grief as it is when it's my money. Imagine if yours was mingled in there, too."

She glanced at him. "You never gave me a first reason."

"Didn't think I had to." He looked out of his window.

Eva noticed that his jaw was tight and his face brown from days spent mowing the orchard without a tractor canopy. "You don't."

She should know better than to argue. She knew Adam was worried about the frost, but instead of encouraging him, she gave him a hard time. She nitpicked.

Why?

Could it be that she cared more for Adam than what was comfortable? She couldn't control him any more than she could her feelings. Her safety shelf moved down a notch when she realized that maybe it was because she loved him.

Adam woke from a knock on the truck window. He checked his watch. Twelve thirty. Again the knock sounded, interrupting a dream he could barely recall. Eva. He rolled down the window. "What are you doing out here?"

"I thought you might want some help lighting the heaters."

He rubbed his eyes. "What's the temp?"

Eva showed him the thermometer. "Thirty-four degrees."

"Wow. That dropped fast." He'd set his cell phone alarm to go off at one in the morning.

Adam planned to check the temp every hour until it was close enough to freezing to light the heaters. Then he'd hook up the giant fan that he and Eva had loaded in the truck's bed to a generator. Every hour he'd blow the air around from different points on the slope of the orchard's hill. It might be a futile attempt, but he didn't want to lose any part of his crop. Not without a fight.

"Hop in," he said.

Eva hoisted a picnic basket between them.

He peeked inside and smiled. "What have we here?"

"Oatmeal cherry caramel cookies, coffee and a sliced chicken sandwich if you're hungry."

Adam reached for a cookie. They were still warm. "You really know how to kill a guy, don't you?"

She was bundled up in a knit hat and an old down ski jacket that had been patched with duct tape. Her eyes looked sleepy. He'd never thought she looked prettier. "What are you talking about?"

"Homemade cookies straight from the oven." He patted the side of his chest where his heart beat with a strong inclination to pull his farm girl close. "Right here, Eva. You're killing me right here."

Her eyes widened and she blushed. "We better get those heaters lit before it gets much colder."

Always business, his Eva. What she didn't say with her lips, her baked goods spelled out a whole lot of caring. For him. He'd offer his heart to those pastry-floured hands of hers if he could. But he'd promised they'd go slow. For both their sakes, he'd honor that promise until the harvest was completed by the end of July. If God allowed the weather to cooperate.

"You going to start the truck or sit there staring at me?"

He swallowed his mouthful of cookie and grinned. "You're awfully cute in that hat."

"And you're silly when you're tired."

"Then be silly with me."

"Like we'll have a ton of fun keeping the orchard warm."

"Why can't we? God will honor our effort."

"And what if He doesn't? Bad things happen." Her brow furrowed.

He knew that as much as she did. "Doesn't mean we stop giving Him our all. That's the true test of faith, isn't it? To keep loving Him when it's tough, even after we've lost what we hold dear."

Too bad he hadn't lived up to his words. Once his mother had died, he gave up on honoring God. Sure, he'd only been a kid, but he knew right from wrong. He purposefully went his own way for years until he was sick to death of the emptiness.

"It's not always easy."

He brushed the crumbs from his fingers. "I know."

Eva's eyes looked black at night. Deep, dark pools of hardened hurt. She was thinking about that guy who'd hurt her. She blamed God, and she still held on to her fear.

He softly cupped her chin. "I've been everywhere doing everything without an ounce of peace at the end of the day. There's nothing worth having without God, Eva."

She stared at him hard, as if weighing the truth behind his words. Eva had what he didn't have— loving Christian parents and a clean life. And yet there was bitterness in her. Fear.

And then she smiled. "Thanks, Adam. For keeping me grateful."

"I'm here for you. I mean, we're supposed to help each other carry the burden, right? When yours gets too heavy, hand it over."

She looked thoughtful a minute, and then her brow cleared and she grabbed a cookie. "Deal. Let's light the heaters before it gets any colder."

"Deal." He exited the truck, and they ignited the first few propane heaters within walking distance.

Then they jumped back into the pickup and drove to each heater placed in the lowest section of the orchard. Lighting them, Adam prayed that God would give him the right words for Eva. The right actions. Plain and simple, he prayed for her. She'd become his prayer habit.

Once the last heater glowed with the bluish heat of propane, they both leaned against her truck and surveyed the sight.

"This might not do a thing." Eva's breath curled white in front of her.

Adam glanced at the clear sky filled with stars and the full moon that hung like a neon sign. A year ago, he'd never have thought he'd be standing in the middle of an orchard with a girl like Eva. He enjoyed being with her. Didn't matter what they did. Work was more fun and life more fascinating when he knew she'd be there, too. She challenged him, but she also made him feel complete somehow.

Like part of him had been missing without her. *His rib.*

The thought made him smile.

He prayed God would protect his crop as he looked down the gentle slope toward the low-lying portion of tart cherry trees. The orchard was aglow from the heaters. "Looks pretty cool, doesn't it?"

"It does."

He wrapped his arms around Eva and rested his chin on the top of her head. After a few minutes of staring at the view in silence, he said, "I'll drive you back to the house."

She snuggled closer. "You're really going to stay out here all night?"

"Unless you have a better idea."

"Do you need my help?"

"Nope. I've got it. I'll set my cell phone alarm and then check the temperature every hour." He knew better than to accept her offer to help.

They climbed in her pickup and headed back to Eva's farmhouse. Before she slipped out of the passenger side, she turned to him. "I'll leave the door open if you need a nap on the couch come morning."

"Thanks."

"Call me if you need me, okay?"

Another delay and he'd ask her to stay out there with him. "Good night, Eva."

She gave him a quick kiss before she slipped out the door and jogged up the steps.

He drove back into the orchard. Turning off the engine, he pulled the quilt around his shoulders, but sleep was far off. Maybe he'd stare down the frost from forming.

Closing his eyes, he asked God for one tiny miracle. *Save the orchard.*

Chapter Thirteen

Eva peeked into the living room where Adam still lay on the couch. Morning sunshine streamed in through the windows and the temperatures climbed. There'd been no hard freeze, just a couple patches of barely discernable frost.

This morning Eva had made Adam breakfast and then she'd gone out to mow after he'd slouched onto the sofa. She wondered if he'd gotten any sleep at all last night. The propane rental had been an unneeded expense, but she wouldn't dream of telling him so. His commitment had struck a chord deep inside her. Making her proud. Adam had the makings of a fine grower.

Puttering in the kitchen making sandwiches, Eva didn't hear Adam's approach. But she felt his arms slide around her waist as he kissed the back of her neck.

"Morning," he whispered.

She laughed and slipped away to fetch lettuce from the fridge. "It's afternoon, sleepyhead. Almost two."

Adam stretched. "Wow. I was out cold."

"Hungry?"

"Yes." His eyes darkened.

Eva needed a work subject to discuss and fast or they'd end up in each other's arms when there was work to be done. "We might have an early harvest if it stays warm, thanks to no freezing last night. At this rate, we'll have sweet cherries to pick for the Fourth of July. Just in time for the Cherry Festival in Traverse City."

"I better follow up with that list of workers your father gave me."

Eva set a sandwich plate and a bag of chips on the table before she grabbed glasses and lemonade. "I can help with that. Who've you called?"

Adam sat down. "A couple guys are already working for a larger orchard. They didn't expect to be hired back once your dad sold."

Eva slipped into her seat. "I'll look over the list."

"Your dad said you wouldn't know the guys he hired the past two summers. You were in New York."

Eva cocked her head and mumbled around a mouthful of sandwich. "How often do you talk to my dad?"

"I don't know." Adam shrugged. "Every week, every couple of days."

"Why are you calling him when you've got me?"

Adam chuckled. "Sometimes your dad calls me to get an update on the orchard. He said you don't give him enough details."

Eva swallowed her irritation, but it lodged in her throat like an underchewed piece of bread. "It's not easy when I hear in his voice how much he misses it."

"He told me that he's glad to be out from under all this."

Eva knew her father. He might put up a good front for Adam's sake, but he missed the farm. It was his livelihood for so long, so how could he not?

"I wish they didn't live so far away." Eva bit into her sandwich even though she'd lost her taste for it. Adam and her father were leaving her out of the loop on purpose. What she couldn't figure out was why.

"What if they spent their summers here?" Adam grabbed a couple more chips.

"That'd be great." Eva smiled.

"Good." Adam returned an even broader smile. Even without sleep, an unshaven chin and hair that stuck out in places, he was the most handsome man she'd ever known.

And loved.

The realization of how deep her feelings had grown warmed her insides. She loved him. But could she tell him? Or should she wait until she knew that he loved her back?

Adam took his plate to the sink and stretched. "Well, I'm heading out to mow."

She smiled at him with her heart feeling as if it had ballooned on her. "I'll be out in a bit. Make sure you take water. It's getting warm out there."

"Will do." He grabbed an apple and kissed her cheek. Settling his hat on his head, he gave her a wink and left.

Humming, Eva folded the throw blanket that Adam had left in a bunch on the couch when she noticed that his cell phone lay on the coffee table. As if on cue, it rang. Should she answer it or let it go to voice mail?

She peeked at the screen. And the name Bob Marsh flashed as it rang again.

Eva picked it up. "Hello? Dad?"

"Eva? I must have dialed the wrong number."

"This is Adam's phone."

"Is he there?"

"No. He's mowing the field. What's up?"

Her dad's pregnant pause made her worry. "Nothing. Tell him to call me."

Now she was really curious. The two men she loved most had something going on behind her back. The fact that they were both hesitant to let her in on it irritated her. "I can give him a message, you know."

She heard her father's chuckle at the other end. "I know you can, honey."

Eva waited. When her father still didn't spill his message, she got mad. "What's going on, Dad?"

"Nothing."

"I don't believe you. You and Adam have this secret society thing going and I'd like to know what it is and why."

"Eva." Her father sighed. "Now you're overreacting. I'm just helping Adam out."

Her hunch that this was more than simple farming tips cut to the quick. "How?"

"The man has a lot at stake. He needed someone he could talk to."

A splinter of hurt dug deep. Why couldn't Adam talk to her?

"Eva? There's something you should know. Your mother was right. She said we should tell you, but Adam wanted it to be a surprise."

Her gut clenched. "What's that?"

"Adam's flying us up to help bring in the harvest."

Eva's mouth went dry. "When?"

"This weekend."

* * *

Hauling herself behind the wheel of her truck, Eva started the engine and pushed the gas pedal too hard. She drove out into the field, jostling in her seat. It was time she got to the bottom of why Adam had left her out of the loop. She drove until she spotted Adam's tractor deep in the orchard gingerly mowing the lanes.

She pulled far enough in front of him so that he'd see her. She slammed into Park and got out, not bothering to shut her door. Classic rock tunes poured from the big John Deere.

Adam climbed down fast, his expression alarmed and full of concern. "What happened? What's wrong?"

"How could you not tell me?" she spat.

Confusion marred his handsome face. "What?"

"Fly my parents up for more than a month's stay without so much as giving me a heads-up?"

His eyes closed for a moment. "Who told you?"

"My dad." She tossed his cell phone at him. "You left this on the coffee table and he called. I saw it was him and picked up. You go to my dad and you go to Ryan, so why don't you talk to me?" She pointed at her chest. "You hired me, remember?"

He took his hat off, ran a hand through his hair and then settled the cap on backward. Dressed in yesterday's jeans and a T-shirt, his arms and face browned by the sun and dark stubble raking the line of his jaw, Adam Peece had never looked so good. Or more at home in the orchard.

He stepped toward her, his hands spread wide in surrender. "I thought you'd be pleased to see them. You said yourself that you wished they weren't so far away."

"That's beside the point—"

He cut her off. "Then what's the point, Eva? Why are you so fired up?"

She sputtered. How did she put to words the betrayal she felt when her dad admitted to Adam's need to talk to someone other than her about the farm? *Their* orchard? "Because there are things I need to do before they get here, like clean my house, grocery shop."

He chuckled as if her concerns were a paltry reason to get mad. "I can help you if it makes you feel better."

She stepped closer. "No, it doesn't make me feel better. You still haven't answered my question. Why do you keep going to my dad and Ryan for confirmation on what I've shown you? You check on everything I do."

"Whoa, hold on a minute. That's not fair."

She glared at him. "Isn't it?"

His face darkened and his blue eyes blazed. "You never expected me to make it, Eva. From the moment I started, you thought I'd bail. You didn't think I had a chance without your expertise. Well, I can figure out some things, too, you know."

She opened her mouth but nothing came out. He was right.

"You've shown me what to do and how to do it, but you never tell me the whys. I need to know the whys. Why wouldn't I seek out second opinions from people I trust to give me a straight answer?"

She inhaled a deep breath. "You don't trust *me?*"

"How can I? You hit me up with a partnership offer before we've had a full season of working together. Do you think I'm stupid? I know how much this orchard means to you."

Her eyes widened. "I've done what you've hired me to do. I can't help it if I doubt your commitment. Look where you come from."

"And you can't see past what you *think* I am, can you?" His voice hardened as he stepped closer.

"Not when you throw money at problems—like those propane heaters, for example."

"Come on, Eva. You know why I did it. I couldn't sit by and do nothing."

She stepped closer and poked his shoulder with her index finger. "Maybe not, but you're flying my dad up here to help you with the harvest because you don't trust my help. Maybe I should give you my two-weeks' notice right now and save you the expense of my salary. You don't need me."

"I do need you, Eva." His voice dipped to a hoarse whisper. "Too much, I'm afraid."

They stood mere inches from each other. In that instant, the fight went out of Eva even though the heat remained. In fact, it cranked up a couple degrees. She'd never quit and Adam would never fire her. They were meant to work this farm together.

Adam moved first, pulling her close.

Eva wrapped her arms around him and hung on. Her knees gave way when Adam's fingers combed through her hair, drawing her head back so he could look into her eyes. He didn't say a word. He didn't have to. He was going to kiss her. And this time, he wasn't holding back.

She didn't want him to.

The contact of his lips against hers made her dizzy. Exhilarated. Nervous. Eva slipped and he supported her by leaning against the wheel of the tractor. The pressure of Adam's lips grew more insistent as he deepened the kiss.

Like a warning flare, caution edged into her brain. *Careful.*

But this was Adam.

She stiffened when the contours of the tire bit into her back. Eva braced against Adam's chest to make more room, but he captured her hands, threading his fingers through hers. He wasn't letting her go.

A sliver of panic pierced her.

Pinned.

For a split second the memory of that awful night with Todd crashed into her mind. She'd been thrown to the ground, the wind knocked out of her. Todd had trapped her against the hard-packed dirt of a two-track. She couldn't breathe.

But this was Adam.

She'd be okay. With some air. She just needed air.

Eva pulled her hands free and pushed at Adam's shoulders. Nothing. Her fingers and toes tingled. Numb.

Adam murmured her name as he kissed her cheek, her jaw, the hollow of her neck, giving her the chance to gulp a few breaths. But she saw stars. She was losing peripheral vision and darkness threatened.

No. She couldn't freak out with Adam.

But it was too late.

She pushed at him when his mouth sought hers again. Shaking like a fruit tree getting picked, she ground out, "Stop it!"

Adam immediately backed away. "Eva?"

She read concern in his eyes, but her breaths came fast and her eyes blurred with tears.

"Talk to me, Eva." He reached for her.

She turned away from him and bent down. Placing her hands on her knees, she struggled to stave off the dizziness that threatened to overtake her. "I can't."

"Sweetheart, it was just a kiss. I wouldn't ever—" His voice carried a hint of panic.

She figured no other girl had ever reacted to Adam Peece's kiss like this. The thought almost made her laugh.

She shook her head, trying to clear it, trying to regain her strength. Her dignity. She saw her truck with the door wide-open. A Led Zeppelin song wailed from Adam's tractor, making everything seem surreal.

She had to get out of there, if only she could make her feet move. Straightening, she whispered, "I'm sorry, Adam. I'm so sorry."

Adam didn't know what to do or how to help her. Eva looked ready to shatter if he dared touch her. He watched her fight tears as her gaze darted from the truck to him and then back to her truck.

His heart broke. He'd rushed her. This was his fault. She'd told him before that she wasn't ready— but the way she'd responded...

He reached out and rubbed her shoulder. "We can get through this."

"I can't, Adam. I want to, but I can't." A tear slipped down her cheek and then she darted for her truck.

"Eva, wait." He went after her.

"Just leave it alone, Peece. Leave me alone." Her voice sounded tight as she slammed the truck door. Then she drove away.

How was he supposed to fix this? He couldn't buy his way out of this one. Adam gripped his forehead and closed his eyes tight when it dawned on him. Had she lied about what had happened to her? Was it worse than she'd let on? He clenched his jaw and felt sick.

Dear God in heaven, show me what to do.

He waited, knowing no clear answer would suddenly appear. It didn't work that way, at least not for him. He walked to the tractor and kicked the tire before climbing in. And then he sat for a long time, stunned.

Not since his mom died had he felt such a blanket of helpless despair wrap around him. What should he do?

There was nothing he could do…

Except pray.

Chapter Fourteen

After a couple hours of mowing, Adam couldn't take any more. He pulled into the barn, shut everything down and closed the big metal door with a rattle and snap. He had to see Eva before he left for his town house. At least talk to her.

Taking the porch steps in two strides, he knocked on the door into the kitchen.

Beth answered. "Hey."

"Is Eva here?"

Her roommate stepped back to let him in. "She's upstairs."

Adam adjusted his hat. "Is she okay?"

Beth looked him square in the eye. "She told me what happened. Adam, I'm so sorry. I think Eva's scared you'll give up on her. Please don't."

He'd never walk away. Not now, not ever. "I don't know how to help her."

Beth gave him an encouraging smile. "Just love her."

"What if that's not enough?"

Adam paced to the kitchen sink and stared out the window that overlooked the side yard and driveway. He could see the lower orchard from here. The very spot he and Eva had worked to save with the rented propane heaters. But their efforts hadn't been needed. God had come through that night. The temperatures had held.

Love was a big step. One he couldn't take until he'd come completely clean with Eva. When she knew the tenuous hold he had on the orchard, she might not want his pledge of forever.

"Eva's the most giving person I know, Adam." Beth's voice interrupted his thoughts. She stood next to him, leaning against the same counter.

He turned and gave her his full attention.

"My family moved here when I was in junior high and Eva was the first person to reach out to me. When my dad died in the line of duty my freshman year, my mother lost it. Eva was there for me. She pulled me into the Marsh family and without her and her family, I don't think I would have made it through high school." Her expression was serious, as if this wasn't something she talked about often.

Adam could easily imagine Eva's determination in helping her friend. It was no wonder they'd remained close.

"Todd stripped Eva's trusting nature away from her. It hurt to see that part of her shrivel up and die. But I prayed that God would someday send a man who could bring her back to life. And He did. He sent you, Adam. Don't ever doubt that."

Deep down, Adam wondered if that might be true. The power of Beth's prayers blew him away. God had drawn him here before he'd even turned his life around and it humbled him.

"Thanks, Beth," he said.

She gave him a quick hug. "I'll tell Eva you're here."

Adam nodded and waited, but his insides churned.

With a straightening of her shoulders, Eva came downstairs. She stuffed her hands into the back pockets of her jeans to keep them from shaking. The saying went that there was cleansing power in tears. Well, she felt as if she'd been scoured with steel wool. Raw, spent and her heart aching for Adam.

"Hey," she said.

The worried look in Adam's eyes confirmed that he was having a hard time, too. He gestured toward the door. "Can we take a walk?"

She nodded. "I think we should."

After such a cold night, the afternoon's warmth still came as a surprise, like a hint of the promised heat to come. This weekend, Memorial Day weekend, was the official opener of summer. And the busiest time for a cherry grower right up until the first week of August.

Silently, Eva walked with Adam around the other side of the pole barn to a picnic table situated on level ground. The view of the orchard was spectacular here, the same vantage point that Adam's sister had admired less than a couple months ago.

Adam sat on the table's top. Resting his elbows on his knees, he looked up at her. "What happened today?"

Eva twirled the end of her ponytail, wrapping it around into a makeshift bun and then stuffing the ends under the elastic holder. "I'm sorry. I…panicked. It was like I had a flashback and it freaked me out."

"Flashback? Of Todd?"

Eva nodded.

Adam's eyes widened with shock and hurt. By the desolation of his expression, he thought the worst. He looked scared. "What did that guy do to you, Eva?"

Looking out over rows of cherry trees with their deep green leaves hiding the developing fruit, Eva swallowed hard. "We were at a party in the woods. Todd and I had walked away from everyone. He'd been drinking. I never should have followed him—" She stopped and looked at Adam.

He reached for her hand and squeezed.

She didn't let go. "He had me pinned, Adam. On the ground. I fought him the best that I could, but he was so much stronger. He had one hand on my throat, choking me while he—" She couldn't say it. Her clothes had been ripped, her flesh bruised.

She shook off the images flashing through her mind. Tried to forget the rage in Todd's eyes when she'd refused him. "I couldn't breathe. I thought I was done for. But Beth found us before he'd gone too far. She helped me get away."

Adam stared at her. "Did you go to the police?"

"No. I wouldn't. Ryan and Sinclair had been under investigation for the accidental death of Ryan's girlfriend a few months before. I couldn't put my folks through that. More interviews, possibly a trial. All I wanted to do was forget it." She wanted him to understand how it was. How helpless she'd felt. Powerless. Why she reacted the way she did today.

"So you buried it." Those blue eyes of his held understanding.

"I wore turtlenecks a month straight, but it was pretty easy to hide. No one guessed what had happened because we were all heartbroken over Sara."

Adam reached for her other hand while images of his farm girl fighting off that brute ripped through his brain. "I'm so sorry."

If he ever saw that guy again, he'd—

Forgive.

The word whispered through his heart, his mind, his very being. That thought hadn't belonged to him. It interrupted his anger and stopped him cold.

How, Lord? How do I do that? How can I show Eva to do that?

Adam knew Eva needed to exercise forgiveness before she'd get closure to what had happened to her. Before she'd be whole.

And he needed to tell her about the property agreement he'd made with his father. Eva deserved to know what he was up against. What they both faced over the next two months. There couldn't be any secrets between them. Not if they hoped to make it.

He felt Eva's tightened hold on his hands, as if afraid to let him go. Did she think he'd leave her? No way.

"What if…" Her eyes were big dark pools of chocolate. "What if I can't handle getting close?"

He gave her a crooked smile. She'd responded to him at first, and she would again in time with healing. Another reason he'd give her space and patience. "We'll figure it out, Eva. If we need to see a counselor, we will. Whatever it takes."

"I need help, don't I?"

"Maybe. Or maybe you need to face this guy."

"Are you crazy?" Fear jumped in and she let go of him, taking a step back. "I can't. I won't."

"As much as I hate it, we've got to forgive Todd before we can move on. Before we can move forward."

"We?"

"This affects me, too. I'll stand with you, whether it's counseling or facing Todd or both. I don't want you to face him alone. You don't have to go it alone."

Her eyes filled and she gave him a wobbly laugh. "I didn't think I had any tears left. You'd do this with me?"

Adam got up from the table and wrapped his arms around her, feeling her wet tears against his cheek. He did nothing more than hold her. Not gently like she'd been spun of fragile sugar ready to crack. He held her tight, with cherishing strength.

He had no intention of letting his farm girl go.

He loved her too much.

Without asking, Adam started to pray, "Dear Lord, You said that where two or more are gathered that You'd be there, too." Adam searched for the right words.

"Go on," Eva whispered.

"Eva and I are standing before You and we need Your help. Show us how to forgive the unforgivable. Give Eva peace and healing so she can find new life in You, Father. Amen."

"Amen." He felt her bury her forehead into his shoulder.

He stroked her back, wondering if maybe he should wait to tell her about the agreement with his dad, but he knew better. Her folks were flying in on Saturday. Two days away. Eva needed to hear the news from him.

"There's something I have to tell you."

Pulling back, she searched his face. "What? What is it?"

"You've been honest with me, and I need to be the same with you."

She looked worried. "Tell me."

He struggled to go on, hating the possibility that he might ruin everything. "I didn't borrow against my shares in Peece Canning Corporation to buy Marsh Orchards like my sister told you."

Eva stepped out of Adam's embrace. Now *she* looked scared. "Then how did you pay for it?"

"My father. He fronted me the money with the agreement that if I don't break even the first season, I'll forfeit the property to him for development."

Eva's eyes widened. "Why, why didn't you tell me before?"

Before they meant something to each other? Before he'd fallen in love with her? He raked a hand through his hair. "At first I thought you wanted me to fail. I couldn't give you any more ammunition.

And then, when I saw how much you loved this place, when I realized how much the orchard meant to you and your dreams, I couldn't tell you. I was afraid I'd lose you. And I couldn't afford that."

"Oh, Adam."

Disappointment seeped from her like a tangible thing he could touch. He felt it hit like a wave washing away his footing, bringing him down.

"There's still so much that can go wrong, preventing us from bringing in a good crop," she whispered.

After last night's vigil, Adam was beat. "I know. That's why I'm flying your parents in this weekend. That's why I stayed in constant contact with your dad and have been ever since closing on the loan. I need all the help I can get."

"And what happens if you break even? What then?"

He smiled at her, but he could tell that she wasn't warmed by it. "I'll cash in my shares, 401K, everything I've got to pay my father off. Then I'll be officially done with Peece Canning."

"Which is what you want, right?"

His eyes narrowed. Considering how often he'd stepped off the path to try something new, he shouldn't be surprised by the uncertainty in her voice. "Yes, Eva. I want to be a grower. This is what I want. And *you* are what I want."

"Then we have to break even."

He couldn't gauge her reaction. But there was a determined glint in her eye that he knew well. Eva wasn't going to let him fail. "That's the plan."

By the time Eva's parents arrived on Saturday, she was more than ready for them. While she cleaned, shopped and baked, Eva knew God wanted nothing less from her than to forgive Todd. She'd been running from it too long. No more excuses. If God had brought Adam into her life to help her do what must be done, then she'd do it. She'd face Todd and be done with it.

But the how and when remained a mystery. She had no intention of seeking him out. At least Adam would be with her if it came down to seeing him at church.

Adam...

His news about losing the orchard lay like a lead ball in her stomach. If she kept busy, she didn't think about it. But then suddenly she'd feel that risk of loss roll around her belly. There was nothing she could do but put up a good front while she worked. But it was hard.

Wiping her hands on a towel, she leaned against the island counter and checked the clock on the wall. Her parents would arrive soon. She'd been baking all morning, while Adam mowed the field.

Laughter on the porch brought Eva's head up as the door burst open. Bob and Rose Marsh crowded into the kitchen, followed by Ryan and Adam carting their luggage.

Eva glanced at Adam. He looked tired and worried. Just like a real grower this time of year. But what if this year was all they had? What then?

"Eva!" Her mom dashed forward with her arms wide.

Eva flew into her mother's warm embrace. She might as well be a kid with a skinned knee failing to be brave. The comfort of resting within those wonderful arms crumbled something deep inside Eva. She clung tighter.

"What is all this?" Her mother patted Eva's back like she did when Eva was little.

Eva retreated with a shaky smile. "I really missed you."

"You'll be sick of us in no time. We're staying the whole summer, you know." Her mother laughed.

"Yeah, I know." Eva went to her father next and was scooped up into a bear hug.

"Hey, are all those cookies for us?" Her father reached for one before he'd even put her down.

"The youth group's having an interchurch function and I volunteered to make cookies. There's enough for you guys to have a couple."

Her mom wasn't any taller than her, but she wrapped her arm around Eva's shoulders. "Put the kettle on and tell me how things are going. Your father's itching to get out in the field with Adam."

Eva gave her mom a quick squeeze before stepping away to make tea.

"Ryan, can you put the bags in our room, please?"

"No problem." Her brother hoisted the luggage and left the kitchen.

Eva set a full teakettle on the stove and then called out to Adam and her father's departing backs. "I'll have lunch ready in an hour or so. Beth will be home by then, too."

Her mother patted the island chair next to her. "Are you sure you're okay having us here?"

Eva sat down. "Yes, I'm very glad."

"But?"

"But nothing." Eva didn't want to cause her parents unnecessary worry by telling them about Adam's agreement with Leonard Peece. It wasn't just a verbal thing, but a full-fledged notarized contract. Adam had shown her everything, including his expenses thus far.

"How are things with you and Adam?" Her mom's eyes gleamed.

Eva chewed her lip when Ryan bounded back down the stairs.

"Don't worry, I'm not listening," he said as he crossed the kitchen floor. "But they're dating."

Eva felt her cheeks heat. "Thanks, Ryan."

"So, your father was right. You're in love with him."

"Mom!" Nothing like beating around the bush.

Eva's mother had always been what her father called a straight shooter.

"I knew it. The minute your father introduced me to him, I knew he'd be perfect for you."

The teakettle whistle blew, saving Eva from having to answer. She popped up and poured steaming water into a carafe. Eva wasn't about to make any plans with Adam until the end of the season. How could she?

And how could her mother have possibly known anything when it came to her and Adam? But Eva's mother knew everything, and that was what made Rose Marsh so charming and infuriating all at once. She spoke her mind, and she was usually right. But this time, she might be wrong.

"Look, Mom, we're taking it slow. One day at a time." She set down the carafe and slipped back into her seat.

Her mother nodded as she fished out a teabag from the canister Eva placed in front of her. "Then you know what's at stake."

Eva froze. "What do you mean?"

Her mother's eyes narrowed. "Eva, did you know that Adam stands to lose the orchard to his father?"

"Yes. I know."

"How do you feel about it?" Her mother dunked the teabag once, twice, three times before draping the tag over the rim of her mug.

"I'm not happy. Not at all. How could I be?"

Her mother reached out and grabbed both of Eva's hands, stilling them. "Before you go any further with Adam, Eva, you must ask yourself one question. Can you love this man if he loses it all?"

A chill took hold of Eva. She'd refused to think about the worst-case scenario as much as possible. It made her sick to dwell on it. It wouldn't happen. It couldn't. But her mother waited for some kind of response. Eva could only answer honestly. "I don't know."

"Well, you better find out because, according to your father, Adam's giving this everything he has. But it might not be enough."

Later that evening, Eva drove her pickup to church loaded with boxed chocolate-chip cookies. The windows were down and the warm night air blew in all around her. Singing along to a blaring radio helped block out what they were up against this season. It kept her from thinking too hard.

Eva pulled into the parking lot. She spied the vans and school buses from other church youth groups that had come for the special event—a speaker to teens had been brought in all the way from Chicago.

Eva parked. Then she grabbed the cookies, stacking the boxes against her stomach in order to carry them. Teenagers opened doors for her all the way down to the basement kitchen and fellowship hall.

On her way back up the steps, a man was coming down. When she recognized the broad shoulders, her heart stopped.

Todd!

He looked surprised to see her, too. "Hey, Eva, are you helping out?"

She shook her head and leaned against the railing for support. "Just dropping off cookies."

"Mind if I walk you back to your truck?" His voice sounded unsure, awkward even, as if he'd been caught unprepared.

So was she. Her fingers went numb from gripping the railing so tight. What was he doing here? She looked around expecting to see his wife. No one.

"I help with the youth at our church in Grand Rapids. Susan is at her parents' house. I was hoping to talk to you if you have time. It'll only take a minute." He hardly looked her in the eye.

Eva tamped down the fear clawing its way up her spine, making her neck itch. She needed to face Todd and extend forgiveness. This was her chance. But she'd make sure they were in plain sight. If she needed to scream, she'd be heard. "Let's go to the parking lot."

Eva followed Todd with her pulse and thoughts racing. What did he want to talk to her about? What could he possibly say to her? And why now when his wife was conveniently absent?

Once they were outside, Eva glanced around, making sure people milled about. It wouldn't be dark for another hour yet. She was at least visibly safe. She watched Todd walk next to her. His bulky size was intimidating.

At her truck, she eyed him with caution. Maybe she wasn't ready for this after all. "Look, Todd—"

"I owe you an apology for what I did." His voice broke and he looked away. When Todd raised his eyes again, Eva was moved by the stark regret she saw—and the shame.

Could it be?

"I have a daughter now." He cleared his throat and then briefly closed his eyes. "When I think of someone putting her in the position I put you, it makes me crazy. It wasn't your fault, Eva. I'm to blame for what happened."

Eva's chest tightened and her knees weakened, but she nodded for him to continue. She'd make him say it. She had to hear him say he was sorry.

Facing him brought it all back, but instead of the nightmare holding her in its frightening grip, she felt oddly disconnected. Was this how it felt to gain closure? Watching the attack roll through her mind's eye as if it had happened to someone else?

"I'm so very sorry. Can you forgive me?" Seeing

Todd shaken made her believe that he hadn't been unaffected. He'd been hurting, too.

She was glad of that.

The opening to let go of the bitterness she'd held on to for so long spanned before her. Todd's eyes begged for her to forgive him, to release him from his actions and tell him it was okay. But it wasn't. All the pain she'd stuffed inside worked its way up from her belly, like bile. She wasn't going to get sick. Not this time. This time she had control.

Part of her wanted to give Todd a tongue-lashing he'd never forget, and another part wanted to beat him down to the ground and make him feel what she had that terrible night.

Either one would be nothing more than an empty gesture. She wouldn't be any further ahead than she was now. And Eva needed to get ahead. She desperately wanted to move on and take a chance with Adam—finally free from fear.

"I forgive you." The words burned as they left her tongue. Her throat scourged from saying them.

Todd's eyes looked bright and watery. "Ever since I came to Christ, I've tried to make amends for the way I treated you. One way is working with youth-group guys. I show them the best way I know how that they need to respect each other, especially the girls. I'll never forget what I did to you."

She wouldn't either. But maybe it wouldn't hold her hostage anymore. "I understand."

"Susan wasn't sure you'd talk to me. I'm grateful you gave me this chance."

Eva tipped her head, relieved that his wife knew about their past. Todd really had come clean. His regret was real. His remorse genuine. She cleared her throat. "I am, too."

He gave her a nod. "Thanks, Eva. I finally feel like the weight is lifted."

Eva took a deep, steadying breath. "Yeah, me, too. Bye, Todd."

As she watched him walk back to the church, Eva realized that he and his wife would probably be in Sunday's service. She wouldn't come close to chatting with them, but maybe this time their attendance wouldn't keep her from going. But it'd be okay to go somewhere else, too, depending on what her parents wanted to do. Either way, she'd talk to Adam about it.

Climbing in behind the wheel, Eva started her truck with shaking fingers. She drove down the road but didn't get far before she had to pull over. Tears blurred her vision and rolled down her cheeks. She'd faced her enemy and won, but it was God's turn and Eva owed Him her contrite heart.

Resting her head on the steering wheel, she released a shuddering breath and prayed.

"Forgive me, Lord, for drifting so far away from You. For blaming You when I needed You. I need You, Lord. Please help me heal."

Wiping her nose on some napkins from the glove compartment, Eva stretched out on the seat and stared at the ceiling above her. She listened to the crickets calling from the high grass. The smell of sweet summer was in the air with the first cut of hay. And God felt close, like He held her in His arms assuring her it'd be okay. He'd never been further than a prayer away.

She didn't know how long she lay there before accepting that the weight really had been lifted. She'd been set free. Was it enough to banish the horrible flashback? Eva didn't know yet. She might still need counseling, but she'd go.

And trust God to show her the rest.

This time, she'd trust God with her life.

Chapter Fifteen

The next few days Adam and Eva worked hard alongside Bob Marsh. They had settled into a daily routine of going over the orchard, verifying proper growth and quality of the green cherries. After checking the flytrap counts, Adam and Eva sprayed the trees while Bob contacted his previous workers. Two college-aged guys were lined up to start work through the harvest. They were in good shape.

But Adam couldn't relax. Not yet.

Eva had been supportive, encouraging even. But every now and then he'd catch her gazing over the orchard with a frown. Watching her worry might as well have been a fist jammed into his midsection. Nothing he did felt like enough. Even his prayers fell short.

After parking the tractors in the pole barn for the evening, Bob slapped him on the back. "A good day's work despite this heat."

Adam looked up at Eva's dad and laughed. Not as tall as Ryan, Bob was still an intimidating figure of a man hardened by years of farm work. "You live in Florida. You're supposed to be used to it."

"Yeah, but there's nothing quite like a hot day in northern Michigan. You've done a fine job so far, Adam. The fruit looks good, the bugs aren't too bad. We'll see."

"Thanks." Adam was grateful to have him here, and Bob looked happy to be back in the field. "Let's go eat."

In the kitchen, Beth, Eva and Rose Marsh chopped vegetables for a Tex-Mex dinner. Their laughter put a smile on Adam's face. He felt at home. This place had become home to him. Eva was his home now.

"Wash your hands," Rose said before they could even think of sitting down.

She was the spitting image of Eva in thirty years. Small and slender, her short, bronze-colored hair had streaks of gray, but her eyes were hazel. Eva inherited her chocolate-colored eyes from her father and Grandma Marsh.

"I'll take the upstairs bathroom," Adam offered so Bob could use the powder room in the laundry area.

Bob gave him a raised brow. "The boy knows his way around."

"He's been working here since February," Eva chimed in.

"Uh-huh." But Bob was grinning at them.

"Don't worry, Mr. Marsh. Eva's been properly chaperoned." Beth gave him a wink.

"Thank you, Beth. Her mother and I can take over from here. Isn't that right, cupcake?"

"Nice, Dad. Real nice." Eva flashed him an exasperated look. But her father's nickname suited her. Small and sweet.

Her parents knew they were dating, but public displays of affection hadn't been practiced in front of the Marshes other than hand-holding. For now, it might be wise to keep it that way.

They'd gone out for ice cream the other night. But instead of hugs and kisses, Eva had told him how she'd faced Todd. He hated that she'd been alone, but the reality was Adam couldn't be more proud of her. They'd talked a lot about their resolve to put their pasts behind them.

He watched Eva standing at the sink and working next to her mother. Eva still wore the same clothes from the field—a pair of shorts with a doubled-up tank top. She was beautiful. His dainty cherry pixie was pretty from the top of her messy ponytailed head down to her bare feet.

The thought of spending his life with Eva, here on this cherry farm, made his heart pump with longing. He had to succeed. Another six weeks and they'd finally know. For now, he felt as if he'd been placed in a holding pen. Relationship limbo.

After dinner Adam pulled Eva onto the porch to say good night. "Thanks."

"For what?"

Adam shook his head. He wanted to tell her how he felt. That once the harvest was in, he wanted to make plans with her, the lifelong kind. But the words stuck in his throat. He couldn't push that on her, not yet. Not until the orchard was safe. "Thanks for hanging with me through this."

Her eyes mirrored the anxiety he carried, but she wrapped her arms around him and held on tight. "It'll work out the way it's supposed to."

He buried his face in her neck.

The screen door squeaked as Bob opened it. "Ah, Adam. You might want to see this. It ain't good."

"What is it?" Adam pulled away from Eva but gripped her hand as they followed her father into the house.

Severe weather warnings for several counties blipped across the bottom of the TV screen. Leelanau County was one of them. Adam's stomach turned.

He let go of Eva's hand and grabbed the remote from the coffee table. He changed the local channel to the weather station and felt like cursing. A mass of severe thunderstorms packed with high winds was rolling through Wisconsin. The massive red and yellow radar image headed straight for them. It'd overtake them in a few hours.

"The lake might weaken the storm's strength," Eva said.

"Maybe," her father echoed.

Adam couldn't tear his gaze away from the TV. "Bob, you mind if I stick around?"

"I'll have Rosie make up the spare bedroom."

"Don't think that'll matter. I doubt I'll be sleeping much tonight."

Eva watched Adam pace the living-room floor only to stop, peek out of the lace curtains and then pace some more. Lightning flashed with brilliant streaks of blue that brightened the room lit with only a couple of lamps. Thunder rumbled in the distance, but the rain hadn't arrived yet. The air hung heavy and still, as if it, too, held its breath.

Adam flipped back to the weather station. They all waited for the close-up radar map of Michigan to flash onto the screen. The storm was coming. And it was big.

"Is there anything we can do?" Adam looked at her dad.

Her father had been the one Adam turned to for answers from the very beginning. Eva tried not to take it personally, but it was tough when Adam hardly looked at her.

"All we can do is wait it out." Her father leaned forward, elbows on his knees. He watched the forecast as closely as Adam did.

"Anyone want some tea?" Eva's mom looked up from her book and peered over the top of her reading glasses.

"We're fine, Rose," her father answered.

Every grower faced the uneasiness of nature's fickle turns. Sometimes for the best, sometimes for the worse. Eva knew how it went. She remembered nights like this as a kid. Her mother used to round them all up—Sin, Ryan and her—and then read to them. Some fairy tale or a story from the Old Testament. Anything to keep them occupied. Anything to keep them from asking their dad questions.

Her father had paced and prayed just like Adam did now.

She smiled at the similar intensity Adam had that was so much like her father. But she might as well not be there for all the help she could give either of them. "I'm going out on the porch."

Adam glanced at her then, his blue eyes troubled, but he nodded.

Letting the screen door close with a snap, Eva sat down in a rocking chair to watch the storm come in. Despite the very real possibility of a bleak outcome, the dark sky was beautifully lit up. The lightning grew more insistent, more colorful and more threatening with every flash.

"Dear Lord," Eva whispered, "this whole thing is in Your hands. Your will be done. I'm trusting You on this."

Sitting quietly, she hummed while she rocked. The sounds of thunder grew louder as the storm barreled closer.

"Are you okay?" Adam stepped out onto the porch.

She turned toward him. "Are you?"

He shrugged. "This is worse than I thought it would be."

"What do you mean?"

"Facing the force of nature, I'm powerless. I might toil, work hard, do everything right and yet one storm can strip it all away. It's that simple and yet complicated."

Eva stood and wrapped her arms around Adam.

He pulled her closer. Taking the elastic holder from her ponytail, he threaded his fingers through her hair and tipped her head back. Searching her eyes, he whispered, "I love you, Eva. I want you to know that."

Warmth spilled into her, but Adam's worry, the finality in his gaze, snatched at her peace. They'd get through this, wouldn't they? "I love you, too."

The wind kicked up suddenly, bending the surrounding maple trees with a whoosh. A folding lawn chair blew over with a bang against the porch and made her jump.

Adam brushed his lips against hers and then grabbed her hand. "Come on, we better get inside."

Eva followed him indoors. Her mother was busy closing windows, trapping the heat of the day inside the house. The ceiling fans ran at full speed, moving warm air around but giving little relief.

Lightning brightened the room again, followed by a deafening crash of thunder. The lights flickered and then went out. The fans slowed to a stop. And then the wind howled as if laughing at them.

The storm had arrived.

Without letting go of each other, Eva and Adam peered outside through the picture window in the dining room. Her parents did the same a few feet away. Even Beth had joined them. After losing power, she couldn't continue with her end of the school year lesson plan.

No one spoke. They just listened. Until a slice of lightning hit nearby and brought down a maple tree with a crack of thunder that rattled the windows. The deafening sound startled them into laughter.

Eva leaned into Adam's embrace as sheets of rain pelted the ground with an unrelenting show of strength. There was nothing they could do but watch their hopes for a successful harvest wash away.

An hour later, as the storm finally rumbled its way east, Adam asked her, "Where are the keys to your truck?"

She knew he wanted to see the damage and the darkness outside didn't matter. He'd want to see what was left even if by the shine of headlights. "I'm going with you."

He waited for her to slip into her shoes. "Bob, we'll be back."

Eva glanced at her folks as she handed Adam her keys. What could she say?

"We'll check out the damage thoroughly in the morning. Things have a way of looking brighter by daylight." Her father wrapped his arm around her mom.

Eva nodded and turned to follow Adam.

Once outside, Eva noticed the scatter of leaves and branches tossed around the lawn. At the far edge of the backyard, the struck maple lay in a splintered heap. Lightning still echoed through the sky with hues of blue and pink.

"Wow," she whispered.

"This doesn't look good, does it?"

"I've seen worse." When she was twelve, a hailstorm had obliterated her father's cherry crop. That year had been bad for every grower. The area's entire supply of cherries was lost.

Silently they climbed into her truck and Adam drove. Bouncing down the lanes of the high portions of the orchard wasn't pretty. They each rolled down their windows to better see what was left, if anything, of their cherries.

Light rain dripped in through the opened windows, but it didn't matter. Devastation surrounded them. Cherry tree branches had been broken, and leaves and cherry clusters littered the ground. The wind had torn the orchard to shreds.

"Still want to be my partner now?" His eyes were red-rimmed and his voice dark with sarcasm. Adam Peece had just given up.

But Eva wouldn't let him. They loved each other. That had to count for something.

He went to get out of the truck, but Eva stopped him. "Yes, Adam. I still want to be your partner."

She grabbed his shirt with both hands and made him face her. Right then, Eva knew the answer to her mother's question with sharp clarity. "For life."

He gently tucked a strand of hair behind her left ear, but his expression remained serious. "Are you talking business or personal?"

She laughed at him then, suddenly giddy with the realization that she'd love Adam forever. Losing the orchard, or even losing her family home, wasn't going to change that. "Do you really think we can have one without the other?"

He gave her a smile that made her toes curl. "Eva Marsh, is that a marriage proposal?"

"There's one thing I know, Peece. I love this orchard, but I love you even more."

He leaned closer. "Then I'll take that as yes."

She stopped him with both hands flat against his chest. She smiled, letting happy tears trickle down her cheeks. "But you haven't given me your answer."

"I will, Eva. I want to give you a ring that'll knock the cute little cherries off your apron." He flipped her hand over and kissed her palm.

She stared at him. "I don't need a fancy ring. All I need is you. No matter what happens or where we end up, as long we stick together and trust God, we'll figure it out."

He kissed the underside of her wrist. "We have a lifetime ahead to figure it out. We don't have to rush."

Eva swayed closer. "But we will get married."

"Yes, we'll definitely do that." His face shone with happiness when a flash of distant lightning lit up the sky. Rain still dripped into the truck and the muggy night air carried the smell of wet grass.

None of that mattered when Adam kissed her.

Eva kissed him back.

And this time, she wasn't afraid.

Epilogue

The following May at the height of cherry blossom time, Eva's wedding day dawned warm and sunny. The day couldn't be more perfect. And she felt perfect.

Her mother stepped back and smiled into the mirror. "Sinclair's finally here. Eva, are you ready?"

Eva clicked her tongue and shook her head. Her own brother, the officiating minister no less, was late to his sister's wedding. Typical Sin.

She took another peek at her reflection and smiled.

Her wedding dress was soft and billowy, making her feel like a cherry blossom fairy. Considering the wreath of flowers on her head, all Eva needed were wings. But then she was already floating on air.

"I've never been more ready in my life," Eva said.

Adam and Eva had been busy ever since that

June storm cost them a third of their cherry crop. Straight-line winds had ripped up the orchard on high ground, but the low-lying areas had been spared. Other growers weren't so fortunate. With the cherry supply low and demand high, Adam sold enough quality fruit to break even. The orchard was all his with a promise to be theirs after they returned from their honeymoon.

Eva followed her mother down the stairs into the kitchen where her bridesmaids, Anne and Beth, waited. They leaned against the new cupboards Adam had custom-made from the old cherry trees they'd uprooted.

The thoughtfulness of Adam's gift still tugged her heartstrings. He'd brought the warmth of the cherry wood into their home as a reminder of the Marsh growers that came before them. Their legacy.

Eva ran her fingertips across one of the doors and sighed.

"You are so spoiled," Anne said.

Eva smiled at Adam's sister. "I know. But you don't see how hard Adam puts me to work in the field."

"You love every minute," Beth added.

Another truth.

Adam might be a smart businessman, but he was lazy when it came to keeping track of his investments. He had considerable funds left after paying off his father.

And she'd finally obtained her loan.

Together they spent the fall and winter months renovating the second floor above the garage into an apartment for her parents. And the farmhouse had been upgraded with private baths for each upstairs bedroom along with a private innkeeper addition. Marsh House Bed-and-Breakfast would open for the first time after they returned from their honeymoon.

Eva's father stepped into the kitchen and his eyes filled with tears. "Daughter of mine, you're beautiful."

"Thanks, Dad." Eva's throat grew tight. She glanced at her mom, whose eyes were also shining bright.

Her parents planned to live as snowbirds. After wintering in the Keys, they'd return to LeNaro and help in the field and house. Everyone was truly happy.

Eva linked arms with her mom and dad. "Let's go get married."

Walking toward the blooming orchard, Eva spotted Adam. He stood near a white iron arch draped with flowers and bows compliments of her aunt Jamee. Ryan and Uncle Larry stood with him.

The breeze fluttered a few blossom petals around her groom and, once again, Eva was taken by how handsome he looked. There was no doubt that her cherry-orchard Oberon belonged right here. They both did.

Eva didn't hear the harp music playing, nor did she notice the guests seated in neat rows of white chairs. Walking toward Adam, she focused on the intensity of his laser blues.

She hardly heard Sinclair's words until he asked the final, most important question of the ceremony. "Eva Marie Marsh, do you take Adam Leonard Peecetorini as your wedded husband?"

Eva threaded her fingers through Adam's. The hint of his woodsy cologne mingled with the scent of cherry blossoms overhead. "I do."

Her oldest brother smiled. "Adam, do you take Eva as your wife?"

"You bet I do." An enthusiastic Adam leaned forward for the kiss.

Laughter rippled through the audience.

Even Sinclair chuckled. "Then I pronounce you Mr. and Mrs. Peecetorini. Go ahead and kiss your bride."

Eva thought it'd be a simple smooch like they'd discussed, but Adam surprised her with a full sweep and dip as he kissed her senseless.

Applause from their guests drowned out her gasp.

When they finally broke for air, Eva spotted one of Uncle Larry's honeybees land on the flowers pinned to Adam's lapel.

Adam saw it, too, but he didn't panic. He watched the bee for a moment until it flew away. And then he looked at her. "A fitting christening, don't you think?"

Her heart swelled with pride and she nodded. "I love you."

"I love you more." Adam drew her close.

Eva had never felt more cherished or blessed. They'd made it through the first of many seasons yet to come.

And a lot of dreams yet to be fulfilled.

* * * * *

Dear Reader,

Thank you so much for picking up a copy of my book SEASON OF DREAMS. I've always held farmers in my heart as heroes. I'm enamored with the Leelanau County area of Michigan, so creating a cherry-growing hero was a natural fit. Playing with the Adam and Eve metaphor was fun, but the story didn't start there. A long time ago, I heard about a wealthy business owner's son. He was destined to become a romance novel hero—and so I tucked him away for someday. That day dawned with Adam, a man who didn't trust women. And just like in the book of Genesis, Eva's character came from Adam's. Eva is his perfect helpmate, complete with serious trust issues of her own. I hope you enjoy reading their journey to love and wholeness through faith as much as I enjoyed writing it.

I'd love to hear from you. Please visit my website at www.jennamindel.com or drop me a note c/o Steeple Hill Books, 233 Broadway, Suite 1001, New York, NY 10279.

Many Blessings,
Jenna Mindel

QUESTIONS FOR DISCUSSION

1. The book opens when the orchard is dormant and in need of pruning to spurt new growth and let in light. Eva is spiritually dormant. How does God use Adam to shed light into Eva's darkened spirit?

2. Eva experienced a real problem many young women face. Date violence statistics are shocking, with up to half of college-aged males admitting that they've perpetuated one or more sexual assaults during their college experience. Of these men, seventy-five percent were involved in drinking or drugs prior to the incident (as cited by www.ncvc.org/dvrc). What can the church community do to combat this problem? How should Christians address this?

3. Eva blamed God for His lack of protection. Why is it that we tend to blame God when bad things happen to us?

4. Eva held on to her fear and she refused to extend forgiveness. This blocked her ability to find peace. Is there anything keeping you from experiencing God's peace?

5. Adam walked away from family expectations to follow his dream of becoming a farmer. Does God give us our dreams or does He honor our pursuit of them? Or both? What if our dreams are not financially practical—should we still pursue them? Is there anything holding you back from realizing a dream?

6. Adam made peace with his empty past by returning to his faith. The Bible promises a peace that surpasses all understanding if we'd stop worrying and pray for everything. What worries can you turn over to God?

7. Harboring unforgiveness often harms the person wronged far more than the wrong-doer. Eva needed to face her attacker to gain closure and overcome her fears. Can forgiveness be extended without a face-to-face confrontation? If so, how? And what might be the advantages of each?

8. Romans 8:28 tells us that all things work together for good to those who love God and are called according to His purpose. How did this happen for Adam and Eva?

9. Adam and Eva each had their own trust

issues when it came to relationships. What small steps did they take that demonstrated the strengthening of their friendship into something more?

10. Adam and Eva had a dream setting for their wedding. Where's your favorite place to get married?

LARGER-PRINT BOOKS!

**GET 2 FREE
LARGER-PRINT NOVELS
PLUS 2 FREE
MYSTERY GIFTS**

Larger-print novels are now available...

YES! Please send me 2 FREE LARGER-PRINT Love Inspired® novels and my 2 FREE mystery gifts (gifts are worth about $10). After receiving them, if I don't wish to receive any more books, I can return the shipping statement marked "cancel". If I don't cancel, I will receive 6 brand-new novels every month and be billed just $4.74 per book in the U.S. or $5.24 per book in Canada. That's a saving of at least 24% off the cover price. It's quite a bargain! Shipping and handling is just 50¢ per book in the U.S. and 75¢ per book in Canada.* I understand that accepting the 2 free books and gifts places me under no obligation to buy anything. I can always return a shipment and cancel at any time. Even if I never buy another book, the two free books and gifts are mine to keep forever.

122/322 IDN FC79

Name	(PLEASE PRINT)	
Address		Apt. #
City	State/Prov.	Zip/Postal Code

Signature (if under 18, a parent or guardian must sign)

Mail to the **Reader Service:**
IN U.S.A.: P.O. Box 1867, Buffalo, NY 14240-1867
IN CANADA: P.O. Box 609, Fort Erie, Ontario L2A 5X3

Not valid to current subscribers to Love Inspired Larger-Print books.

**Are you a current subscriber to Love Inspired books
and want to receive the larger-print edition?
Call 1-800-873-8635 or visit www.ReaderService.com.**

* Terms and prices subject to change without notice. Prices do not include applicable taxes. Sales tax applicable in N.Y. Canadian residents will be charged applicable taxes. Offer not valid in Quebec. This offer is limited to one order per household. All orders subject to credit approval. Credit or debit balances in a customer's account(s) may be offset by any other outstanding balance owed by or to the customer. Please allow 4 to 6 weeks for delivery. Offer available while quantities last.

Your Privacy—The Reader Service is committed to protecting your privacy. Our Privacy Policy is available online at www.ReaderService.com or upon request from the Reader Service.

We make a portion of our mailing list available to reputable third parties that offer products we believe may interest you. If you prefer that we not exchange your name with third parties, or if you wish to clarify or modify your communication preferences, please visit us at www.ReaderService.com/consumerchoice or write to us at Reader Service Preference Service, P.O. Box 9062, Buffalo, NY 14269. Include your complete name and address.

Love Inspired®
SUSPENSE

RIVETING INSPIRATIONAL ROMANCE

Watch for our series of edge-
of-your-seat suspense novels.
These contemporary tales
of intrigue and romance
feature Christian characters
facing challenges to their faith...
and their lives!

AVAILABLE IN REGULAR
& LARGER-PRINT FORMATS

For exciting stories that reflect traditional values,
visit:
www.ReaderService.com